Fox

Also by Lee Hoffman

THE VALDEZ HORSES
WEST OF CHEYENNE
LOCO

Fox

LEE HOFFMAN

Doubleday & Company, Inc.
Garden City, New York
1976

All the characters in this book are fictitious, and any resemblance to actual persons, living or dead, is purely coincidental.

Library of Congress Cataloging in Publication Data

Hoffman, Lee.
    Fox.

    I. Title.
PZ4.H6975F. [PS3558.O346] 813'.5'4
ISBN: 0-385-11035-9
Library of Congress Catalog Card Number 75–21229

To Carolyn and Fred Featherstone
and The Port Charlotte Cultural Center

CHAPTER 1

The man who presently called himself James R. Todd
stepped down from the stagecoach and surveyed Stick City
critically.

It looked a lot like the town he'd had breakfast in. A lot
like the town where he'd had dinner the day before. A lot like
every other sunbaked cow town the stagecoach had passed
through on its way from the railroad. It was tucked into a
shallow basin that held the early summer heat trapped. Not a
thought of a breeze stirred the dust. Nothing about the place
appealed to his appreciation of comfort, elegance, and cash.

The coach had stopped in front of the town's only hotel. It
was a two-story building with ornate galleries. The ground
floor was occupied by a dining room and a saloon, with the
lobby shouldered in between them. The dining room had a
CLOSED sign in its window. The saloon was open for business.
A few horses stood hipshot and head-hung in the heat at the
hitch rail. A bluetick hound slept soundly in the shade of one
horse. An old geezer with a tobacco-stained beard slept
soundly on the bench by the saloon's batwings.

Todd spotted the bank on the next corner down. It squatted there, a dull red brick toad of a building. The wide door,
angled across the corner of the building, was open. A man
stood in the shadowed doorway. As Todd glanced toward
him, he stepped back and disappeared.

Todd nodded slightly to himself.

The rest of the main street was lined with the usual assort-
ment of false-fronted shops and offices. A barn of a livery stable, weather-beaten and unpainted, marked one end of the
business district. The other end petered out in private houses.

None of it looked of much interest, except possibly the crowd that was gathered on the walk peering into the building labeled STICK CITY SENTINEL. Whatever they watched inside the newspaper office had distracted them from the arrival of the coach. Only a few listless bystanders had gaped at Todd as he alit.

In a place like this, he thought, the arrival of a well-attired stranger should be news. Worth attention. The meager audience disappointed him.

With a muttered comment, the coach driver tossed down Todd's traveling cases. Todd didn't bother to reply. He looked around for a porter of some kind. There didn't seem to be any. Sighing, he picked up the cases himself and started for the hotel.

A balding man in shirtsleeves, bare of vest, collar, and cravat, detached himself from the crowd at the newspaper office and hurried to meet Todd. He caught up at the hotel door, paused to let Todd enter first, then followed.

The lobby was small. To Todd's right, the wall was taken up with a staircase to the upper floor. To his left there was a horsehide sofa flanked by tarnished brass spittoons, and an urn holding the mortal remains of a long-deceased rubber plant. Ahead of him, a high desk held a register, a penstand and inkwell, a clutter of papers, and an open copy of the Stick City *Sentinel*.

Todd set down his cases and turned to face the man who followed him.

"Can I help you?" the man asked, eying Todd in speculation.

"I'd like to see the manager, if you please." Todd's voice was soft and pleasant, his enunciation precise. He spoke with a hint of a drawl, just a suggestion of old southern aristocracy.

"I'm him," the balding man said. "Will Ralston. I own this place."

"James R. Todd of Richmond, Virginia." Todd held out a hand. There were still traces of calluses on it, but no more than an active gentleman might honestly come by. Todd had spent hours soaking his hands, rubbing them with creams and oils like a woman, to soften them and wear away the embedded dirt stains.

He wore a small gold ring on the fifth finger of his left hand, and a matching pin in his black silk cravat. His shirt was of finespun white linen, as was his stiff collar. His suit was dark gray Cheviot, tastefully custom tailored and far too warm for the weather here. His shoes were black calf gaiters, his hat black fur in the planter style. His dark hair was carefully, conservatively cut. His beard, a trim Vandyke, showed a few threads of premature gray. It accented the hard angularity of his jaw and the knife-sharp lines of his mouth. The total effect was of old-fashioned dignity, suggesting more years than he could actually claim.

He was too well dressed for a common drummer, too conservatively dressed for a common gambler. His appearance and bearing bespoke affluence and gentility. Impressed, Ralston pumped the outheld hand and smiled. "It's a pleasure, Mr. Todd. A real pleasure. What can I do for you, sir?"

"A parlor suite, perhaps." Todd's tone was wistful, as if he doubted the hotel could adequately supply his wants.

In his years as an innkeeper, no one had ever asked Ralston for a parlor suite before. No house he'd kept had boasted a parlor suite. "I—uh—I could give you a couple of adjoining bedrooms."

"No." Todd sighed. "If there aren't any suites, I suppose a simple bedroom would suffice. Something in the back, away from the street noise and filth."

"Yes, sir." Ralston scurried around the desk and scowled at the rack of keys. Except for the numbers on the tags, the keys were identical. He decided that a room over the restaurant would be quieter than one over the saloon. Choosing a key, he said, "I've got a real fine bedroom for two dollars a day."

Todd nodded as if price were of no consequence.

"Will you be staying long, sir?" Ralston wondered if he should have asked three dollars a day. But it was too late for that now. He flipped open the register, dipped a pen, and held it toward Todd.

"Until Saturday, I suppose," Todd said as he signed the book. "I understand there isn't another coach out until then."

"There's Bill Long's coach goes through to Dadeston on Tuesday and Thursdays, comes back again Wednesdays and Fridays."

"Does it connect with the railroad?"

"No. It connects with another coach line. I expect you could eventually get to the railroad on it. But the only coach goes direct is on Saturdays. It's hard to get to the railroad from here."

"It isn't easy to get here from the railroad," Todd commented, brushing at the dust on his hat. Despite the closed side curtains, the coach had filled with dust. It had filtered in, seeping through his clothing. He could feel it caked in the sweat on his body. He longed for a bath.

"You in Stick City on business or pleasure, Mr. Todd?" Ralston was asking.

"Business." Todd wondered if anyone ever came to Stick City on pleasure. The idea of a resort here seemed ridiculous. But it wasn't his idea. He replaced the hat, then drew a kerchief from a pocket and swabbed at his face.

Ralston picked up Todd's traveling cases and started for the stairs. "Might be you're looking for somebody in particular around here?"

"Perhaps."

"Might be I could help you find 'em."

Todd didn't answer. Instead he said conversationally, "There seemed to be some unusual activity at the newspaper office when the coach arrived."

"Uh huh. A fistfight." Ralston grinned as he answered.

"A fistfight?" Todd sounded taken aback at the idea. A gentleman might indulge in fisticuffs as a sport, but never to settle an argument.

"Uh huh. Don Edmund, editor of the paper, and Cole McRae from the Pitchfork. Edmund wrote an editorial laying into Pitchfork for damming up Stick Creek, and Cole come in and poked him one for it. I expect Edmund will have himself one hell of a shiner tomorrow. No love lost between them two, there ain't."

"I take it this Pitchfork is a ranch," Todd said as he followed Ralston up the stairs.

"Amos McRae's place. Cole's his boy. Amos lost his older boy on a trail drive a couple of years ago. Lost the youngest with a fever when he was still a baby. Just got Cole and that daughter of his left now."

"Is Pitchfork a large ranch?" Todd asked, although he already knew the answer.

"Biggest around. Only, Edmund figures Amos wants to make it even bigger. He says Amos wants to dry up the little ranchers and run them out. Take their range over himself."

"You think Mr. Edmund is right?"

"I don't know," Ralston said as he led Todd into a bedroom. He set down the cases and wiped his face with the back of a hand. "Amos always seemed like a fair, decent man. I never heard of him doing his neighbors wrong. But what Edmund says makes a lot of sense. The more a man gets, the more he wants. Amos has his whole place free and clear and he's got other fellers in debt to him. They say a big frog will gobble up little frogs, and I reckon Amos is about as big a frog as we got around here. Still, he ain't never seemed like a bad sort."

Todd smiled slightly to himself. He had known some extremely big frogs who seemed like extremely nice people. But he had never yet met one who wouldn't swallow every little frog within reach and then move on, hunting more. But even a big frog was no match for a fox.

"This room do?" Ralston asked him.

The room was large enough to contain its array of furniture without being cramped. There was a brass-steaded bed, a golden oak dresser with a lyre-frame mirror, a matching wardrobe, a commode with the usual complement of crockery, a wooden rocker with a pillow in the seat, and a brass cuspidor. A print hemp carpet covered most of the floor, and roller blinds graced the windows. All in all, it was better than he had anticipated.

But the expression on his face showed a vague distaste. "I had hoped—" he began. He cut himself short. He gave Ralston a small smile that was all politeness, nothing more.

"It's the best I got," Ralston allowed apologetically.

"Quite satisfactory," Todd said. "And the bath?"

"Right next door at the barbershop."

"Haven't you a tub?"

Ralston shook his head. "Nobody ever asked me for one before."

This was really primitive country, Todd thought. Almost as primitive as the slums of New York City. But he would make do. He had made do with far worse. In dismissal he said, "Thank you."

Ralston hesitated, curiosity burning in his eyes. "Is there anything else you'd like, Mr. Todd?"

"No. Thank you."

"The dining room will be open to serve supper at six."

"Thank you," Todd said again, in precisely the same tone of dismissal.

Ralston gave up and left.

The keylock with its common key was pointless, next to useless. A child with a bit of wire might have opened it. But there was a barrel bolt on the inside of the door. Todd slid home the bolt, then went to a window and looked out.

Directly under him, a small shed jutted from the hotel building. Its roof was less than six feet below the window sill. He studied it, then nodded to himself. It could be an adequate way out if a man had to leave the hotel room suddenly.

He had never given much thought to emergency exits in the past. Was he growing more cautious as he grew older? he wondered. Or was he losing his nerve?

It was this damned place, he told himself. This hot, dusty little ragtag of a town. It depressed him. Thinking of the rooftops of Paris, he looked across the alley. It was lined with outbuildings and plank-fenced back yards. A milk cow browsed in one yard. Chickens scratched in others. A small suggestion of a breeze brought him the aroma of hogs.

There were more houses in the distance. Some were trim behind neat, whitewashed fences. Some were little more than slab shanties. They dotted the slope rising behind the town. A steeple identified a church half hidden in a grove of cotton-woods. A wheel-rut road twisted past various gates and on up to disappear over the top of the slope. Two young boys in nothing but short breeches, riding double on a gray mule, headed lazily up the road. Enviously, Todd wondered if they were heading for a swimming hole.

Todd hadn't dipped into a swimming hole—not the natu-ral, back-country kind—since the last time he ran away from the foundling home. That had been a long time since. But in later years there had been tile-lined private pools, lavish spas, exclusive seaside and lakeside resorts.

And now this poor excuse for a hotel didn't even have a tin bathtub.

Stepping away from the window, Todd slipped off his coat and vest. He undid the collar and tie and put them on the dresser. Then he peeled out of the shirt that was sweat-glued to his body. With a muttered curse for the miseries of coach travel, he rubbed both hands at the stiffness in his neck.

The dresser mirror had been tilted down for someone quite a bit shorter than Todd. He adjusted it and frowned at his image. The face was drawn, the cheeks hinting at gauntness. The dark eyes were too hard, too sharp. There was nothing left in that face of the boyish cheer, the bright, eager look of guilelessness, that he had seen a few long years before in the mirrors of Versailles. No, this face was hardly as effective a mask as that had been.

The shoulders were broader now, the muscles hard-planed like some athletic sculpture. A flawed sculpture. The scar of an old bullet wound was an ugly blotch against his skin.

Turning, he looked over his shoulder at the reflection of his bare back. It masked nothing. It betrayed him. The whip scars were still clear. He wondered if they would ever fade away.

With a sigh, he abandoned the reflection and sprawled on the bed. It wasn't as bad as he had anticipated. The mattress was stuffed with moss and only sagged a little. Hardly eiderdown, but a damn sight better than rotten corn shucks.

After a few minutes rest, he reminded himself that there was work to be done. With luck, he might actually complete his business in Stick City in time to leave on next Saturday's coach. But he doubted it. More likely he would have to stay until the following Saturday. It might even drag on until the Saturday after that.

He groaned aloud at the thought of being stuck in Stick City that long.

Hauling himself off the bed, he squatted and unlocked one of the traveling cases. The clothing was packed on top. There were two fresh shirts, two sets of smallclothes, and several collars. Underneath, to add bulk and weight, were old newspapers and a few rocks.

He took out a shirt, a collar, and smallclothes, then relocked the case. There was room enough under the bed for him to shove both cases out of sight. He hoped no picklocks worked this hotel while the guests were out. He might have some trouble explaining his luggage. But, then, a picklock could hardly demand an explanation, could he?

He dressed again in the travel-stale clothing he had arrived in. Then he made an inconspicuous bundle of the fresh clothes. Carrying it, he locked the door behind him and went downstairs.

CHAPTER 2

There was already a customer occupying the barber's single chair when Todd walked into the shop. A man who drummed his fingers on the arm of the chair as the barber carefully applied a leech just below his left eye. Todd thought he might be the newspaperman, Don Edmund. Ralston had said Edmund got a fist in the eye.

The man in the chair was an anomaly in this dingy cow town. His shirt was linen. His vest and trousers were well tailored, and under a thin layer of dust, his boots had a high polish. They were of fine calf and well kept. His thick black hair was pomaded and carefully combed. His mustache was small and trim, with each hair in place. He smelled of lilac water.

Once the bloodsucker was at its work on the customer's cheek, the barber turned to greet Todd. In a glance, his gaze traveled from Todd's hair to his beard to the bundle of clothing he carried. Proud of his acuteness, the barber grinned as he asked, "A bath, sir?"

"Yes. Warm, if you please." Todd hoped it was possible to get warm water here. Remembering tales he had heard of these primitive places, he added. "*Fresh* water, if you please."

"Of course," the barber agreed. Excusing himself to both Todd and the man in the chair, he hurried to the back room to light a fire under his Patented Volcanic water heater.

As the leech filled its gut, the man in the chair peered through one eye at Todd. The eye was so dark that there was no apparent delineation between iris and pupil. The light that glinted in it was mischievous. Or perhaps diabolical. Todd wasn't sure which. He gave the man the quick nod of

one stranger to another, and settled on the bench by the
window to await his bath.

A copy of the Stick City *Sentinel*, dated the previous Saturday, lay on the bench. It was folded open to the editorial that
had brought the wrath of Cole McRae down on Don Edmund. Todd picked it up. He glimpsed a shine in the leech
victim's eye that confirmed his guess. The man had to be
the author of the piece Todd was holding.

Todd read the editorial critically. It went well with its author. It was pretty, in a garish, overblown way, as colorfully or-
namental with verbal birds and swirls as an advance copybook
exercise. Worthy of a hell-fire preacher or a medicine-show
professor. It was full of implications and devoid of facts. An
attempt to stir up trouble where, otherwise, there might actually be none at all.

When he had finished the editorial, Todd went on to skim
the rest of the paper. It was a weekly. The news from the East
was the usual politics and panic, and old enough that Todd
had heard it already. The local items included such news of
moment as new stock received by a hardware dealer, some
horse sales, the highlights of Reverend Barnard's most recent
sermon, and sundry social notes. The name Millard Samson
caught Todd's eye. It was a comment on a new gown Samson
had brought his wife from New York when he returned from a
recent business trip. The gown, cut in the latest Paris fashion,
had evidently impressed the local ladies.

What were the latest Paris fashions? Todd wondered with
a feeling of bitterness. He had liked Paris. It bothered him
that he would never see it again.

The barber puttered with his tools until the leech, finally
sated, released its grip on its victim. He recovered the creature, dropped it into a glass jar, then dabbed its bite with
alum. "That be all, Mr. Edmund?"

"Yes," Edmund said, rising. As he slipped on his coat,
Todd stole another look at him. He was rather short, but well
built. The restless type who, even in repose, radiated energy.
The type who seemed always intent on proving something.

From his dress and manner, Todd guessed he believed he belonged in some more civilized spot than Stick City.

Edmund paid the barber, gave Todd another nod, and left. His eyes on Todd had been appraising, quick and curious. Well, he'd have his curiosity increased before he had it satisfied, Todd thought.

The barber led Todd into the curtained cubicle that housed the bathtub. He turned over a new bar of soap and a fresh towel and stood there looking as if he'd like to stay and chat.

As much as Todd might want to pump him for information and prime him for gossip, it was impossible. Todd couldn't undress in front of him. The bullet scar was no problem. A gentleman might proudly admit to an affair of honor. But there was no honorable excuse for lash scars. Todd made it clear he wanted privacy.

Disappointed, the barber left.

Todd hung his clothes on the wall pegs and slipped into the tub. The water was warm and relaxing. Very pleasant. Sighing, he leaned back and thought of Saratoga Springs, of White Sulphur Springs, of Baden-Baden and Ems. But especially of Saratoga Springs and his first visit there.

He had been around ten when the Colonel took him out of the foundling home to make a gentleman of him. He had been sixteen when the Colonel decided he was finally ready to be introduced into proper society. The Colonel's careful training had forced a veneer of polish onto him, but under it he was still half wild then. And the young ladies at the spa, the daughters of the rich, had been emboldened by the atmosphere. That year, he thought, had probably been the best year of his life.

Lost in memories, he let his eyes close. And the memories became dreams.

He was awakened suddenly by the voice of the barber. The man was poking a head through the curtains, staring at him. Startled, a little frightened, Todd demanded too sharply, "What is it?"

"You've been in here nigh an hour. I was worried. Are you all right? I never had anybody drown in my bathtub. I wouldn't want it. It'd kind of—uh—give the place a bad name."

Todd realized the man couldn't possibly see his back. Catching a deep breath, he said, "I'm afraid I fell asleep. You know how tiring coach travel is."

"You just come in on today's coach?" the barber said.

Todd didn't doubt he already knew the answer. Word of the arrival of an unusually well-dressed stranger should have spread through the town by now. At least he hoped it had. He hoped all the usual sort of gossip and speculation was spreading.

Nodding, he said, "It'll be out in a few minutes. I'll want a shave and a trim. Now, if you'll excuse me . . ."

The barber lifted his brows. Todd had only a scant stubble around his neat beard, and his hair looked very recently cut. Well cut at that. But business was business. He told Todd, "The chair's empty now. I'll hold it for you."

"Thank you."

When the curtains closed behind the barber, Todd climbed out of the tub. Dressed to the vest, he went out to the chair. As the barber wrapped a cloth around his neck, he made an opening move toward the conversation he wanted.

"I must say, this is an excellent shop. Are you the proprietor?"

"Uh huh." The barber pointed toward a name painted in a corner of the window, showing through in reverse. "That's me. Charlie Nardin."

"James R. Todd of Richmond, Virginia," Todd said sociably. He smiled at Nardin.

Nardin smiled back. Chatting with customers was his favorite part of the business. Chatting with a new arrival in town was a special pleasure. "Glad to meet you, Mr. Todd. Is this your first visit to Stick City?"

"Yes it is."

"It's a real nice place. You'll like it."

Todd could have laughed at that. He would have liked Paris or London, Boston or Washington. Even certain parts of New York. But Stick City . . .

Keeping his expression bland, unmocking, he went on with the conversation. "Have you been here long?"

"Since seventy-three. I came out here on account of the panic back East. I had me a nice little shop in Peoria, only when the panic hit, business fell off bad, so I had to give it up. A lot of my old customers came West, so I figured I'd come too."

"How did you happen to choose Stick City?"

"I didn't exactly choose it." Nardin grinned as he whipped up a lather and spread it on Todd's jaw. "It chose me. I was traveling by wagon, hauling my chair along. I stopped over in Dadeston—that's the county seat, you know—and this feller came up to me and said he was from Stick City and the town needed a barber and would I be interested in coming here. I said I would and I did and I've been here ever since."

"Then business is good here?"

"Good enough. It ain't Peoria, but, then, it ain't bad either." Nardin stroked his razor down the strop and peered at the edge. He was enjoying talking about himself, but he wanted to know more about this stranger. He said, "If you don't mind my asking, Mr. Todd, what brings you to Stick City? I mean, you happen to be passing through? Or you visiting somebody here? Or maybe you figure on settling here?"

"Perhaps," Todd said.

"It's a good town," Nardin went on. "You might say it's not exactly booming like some towns. But it ain't heading for a sudden bust like some of them either. You know what I mean. A good, solid, steady town that'll go on being here for a hundred more years. A good town for a feller to settle in and grow with."

"Then you would recommend investing in this area?"

"I sure would. If I had the money to spare, I'd sure invest."

For a few moments, both men were silent as Nardin concentrated on the close work around the edges of Todd's beard and sideburns. When he had finished that, he wiped the blade and asked, "You thinking of investing in these parts, Mr. Todd?"

"Perhaps," Todd said again, giving the word a cryptic quality.

Nardin waited, hopeful of more information. But Todd offered nothing more. Trading razor for scissors, Nardin snipped at Todd's beard. There wasn't much he could do to it. Todd had trimmed it recently himself.

Nardin cut a few hairs, clicked the scissors industriously, and said, "I know a lot of things what's going on around town. A barber hears things, you know. I generally got a good idea who's getting rich and who ain't. A good idea what might be a good investment. Might be I'd know something that would be helpful to you, Mr. Todd. Like I know a nice house that's going up for sale before long."

"I'm afraid I'm not interested in houses."

"A business, maybe?"

"No."

"Cattle? You could pick up a lot of good cattle cheap right now. Got to do it before it rains, though."

"Not cattle."

"Ain't much else," Nardin said.

"Perhaps there isn't anything here I'd be interested in." Todd's tone was thoughtful. He paused as if he pondered something, then said, "I understand there is only one bank in town."

"It's a good bank. Ain't ever failed."

"I understand that it's privately owned."

"Uh huh. It belongs to Mr. Millard Samson. A fine gentleman. I don't expect he'd be interested in selling the bank, if that's what you're thinking of."

"No." Todd laughed lightly, sincerely amused. "I wasn't thinking of buying the bank."

"Then what the Sam Hill—!" Nardin bit back his frustration. "Excuse me, Mr. Todd. I know it ain't none of my business, but you sure as hell make a man curious just what you got in mind."

Nardin was gesturing with the scissors. Todd looked significantly at them. "Are you finished with me?"

"I reckon so," Nardin allowed. He put down the scissors. "Bay rum?"

"No. Just talc, if you please." Todd replied.

Nardin gave him a few dabs of powder, then held up a hand mirror. He looked into it and nodded his approval.

When he had slipped his coat on again, Nardin brushed him down. He looked at himself in the big wall mirror then. The bath, the fresh shirt and collar, and the brushing had helped. Once again, he seemed the very picture of a respectable gentleman. He paid Nardin, and started for the door.

Over his shoulder, he said, "Water, Mr. Nardin. That's what I'm interested in."

"Water?" Nardin grunted. "That's one thing we sure as hell ain't got enough of around here to spare."

Smiling to himself, Todd strolled on up the street.

When a man wanted rumors to grow, there were logical places to plant the seeds. From the barbershop, he went to the office of the Stick City *Sentinel*.

The building was an ordinary one-story false-front. Its door was propped open with a box of battered type. Inside, a counter with a hinged flap at one end stretched from wall to wall, barring the casual visitor from the press.

The press dominated the shop. It was a massive Clymer Columbian, sitting under a grimy skylight like some mechanical idol in its temple. The counterweight atop it was in the form of an eagle. The eagle had lost a wing. A horseshoe tied to its neck made up for the missing weight. Someone had touched up its eyes and mouth with white paint. It seemed to be staring balefully at Todd.

He gave it a wink.

A lean young man with a great deal of Adam's apple, and an ink smear on his cheek, was at a type frame. A composing stick was in his hand. His fingers flew across the type case, setting text. The fingers never faltered as he glanced at Todd.

Edmund was at a desk in a corner, his coat off and black rubber protectors drawn over his sleeves. He was scribbling with the stub of a pencil when Todd walked in. He finished the line he was writing before he looked up. Cocking a brow at Todd, he rose and came to the counter.

"Good afternoon," he said. His voice was very deep for the size of him. There was a suggestion of a nasal twang, as if he had trained himself out of some northeastern accent that refused to leave him altogether. "May I help you?"

"You are Mr. Edmund, the editor, are you not?"

"I am."

"A pleasure, sir. I am James R. Todd, newly arrived from Richmond, Virginia. I understand there is an old Indian holy place, a mineral spring of some kind, in this vicinity. I am hoping that you can tell me how to reach it."

"Are you an anthropologist, Mr. Todd? Should I address you as Professor?"

"No, not that." Todd hesitated long enough to be certain Edmund was aware of the pause. He glanced at the compositor. The man's hands were still now, and his eyes were on Todd. He seemed fascinated by the conversation. Todd went on, "I am simply a traveler in search of out-of-the-way sights of interest. I heard about the spring and thought I might like to see it."

Edmund's mustache twitched in a hint of a skeptical smile. "There isn't much to see. It's just a hole full of water. It's hardly worth the trip up from here."

"I should like to see it and decide for myself."

"It's in the badlands, on Pitchfork range. I wouldn't recommend going there alone. If you insist on going, I'd be glad to guide you there myself."

"Oh, no!" Todd gave the words too much emphasis. "I couldn't impose on you."

"It wouldn't be an imposition at all."

"No! No, I really couldn't."

Edmund's eyes searched Todd's face. He was certain there was more to Todd's inquiry than Todd was admitting. Rather smugly, he said, "Well, it isn't hard to find. You ride out the wagon road back of town. You'll cross a bridge over a gully with a trickle of water in the bottom. That's Stick Creek. Follow it about five miles into the badlands. You'll come to a game trail, an old Indian trail really, that passes an unusually tall rock formation that looks a little like an old woman. She's called The Squaw. Turn left past her and stay on the path. It'll take you to the spring. It's about a ten-mile ride from the bridge. Some of it is rough traveling, but the trail's clear enough."

"You wouldn't recommend making the trip today?"

"No. You'd hardly be able to get there and back before nightfall. You wouldn't want to be in the badlands after dark."

"I suppose not," Todd said. He thanked Edmund for the directions and left. As he walked out, he was aware of the compositor still staring at him.

The compositor wasn't the only one. Walking down the street, Todd attracted covert glances. And a few overt ones. He wondered what the people were speculating about him. And how long it would take the rumors to reach the Pitchfork ranch. He hoped they'd be there by morning.

CHAPTER 3

The new day dawned hot and sticky.

Todd lay awake awhile, thinking of what was to be done that day. He felt none of the old excitement, no eager sense of challenge. This time it seemed to be nothing more than a job. Less distasteful than shoveling manure, but just a job. He wondered what he would do when it was over.

Spend the money, he supposed, and then look for more. But he couldn't spend it in the old ways in the old places, among the people he had once known. No, not now that they knew him. Well, there were other places, and people who didn't know him. There was a life of some kind worth pursuing somewhere. With money in his pocket, he would be able to find it. Now he had to concern himself with getting the money.

Rising, he went to the window and leaned out to scan the sky. Not a hope of a cloud. Nothing to suggest any relief from the heat.

As he dressed, he thought of the local people strolling in public in their shirtsleeves. They didn't even bother with collars in weather like this. As he buttoned on the stiff linen collar, he wondered why it was that the more genteel a man claimed to be, the more discomforts he imposed on himself. Even in hell, a proper gentleman would keep his coat on.

The dining room was open when he got downstairs. He ate a light breakfast, finding little interest in the food. He was aware of the glances others in the dining room gave him, and of more stares as he walked down the street toward the livery stable.

The livery barn was an adjunct of the blacksmith shop. Its

keeper was at the forge when Todd arrived, shaping a shoe for an ugly, ewe-necked, skewbald gelding that was trussed into a heavy framework, its hoofs tied securely. It rolled angry eyes and bared its teeth at the sight of Todd.

The smith looked angry, too. There was a fresh red welt on his bare chest where the little horse had managed to land a kick before it was laced into the cradle.

The smith was a stocky, middle-aged man. He looked Todd down the way he might look at a horse offered for sale. One he didn't think he'd buy. His own hands were horn-hard, thick from rough work. He eyed the softness of Todd's hands resentfully as he asked what Todd wanted.

"I'd like to hire a saddle mount," Todd said.

The smith shook his head. "You want a rig. Nice little mare between the shafts."

A rig would have been more appropriate to Todd's attire, but it wouldn't have gotten him up the trail Edmund described. Todd repeated, "A saddle mount."

"You do, do you?"

"I do."

"A nice little mare?"

Todd understood the implication that he wouldn't be able to handle anything more spirited than a lady's mount. He flicked his tongue over his lips, and said, "I want a handy, sure-footed mount with a mouth that hasn't been ruined yet. One capable of carrying a man."

The smith looked at him a moment longer, then grunted, "Dollar a day, pay in advance."

Todd handed over a dollar.

Turning his back, the smith walked into the barn. When he came out, he was leading an animal even uglier than the beast trapped in the shoeing rack. It was a pony, hardly chest-high to Todd, with a mass of white saddle scars on its back, and more scars from spurs on its flanks. It stood splay-legged, its head drooping, its ears aflop.

Todd lifted a brow at it and told the smith, "I'd prefer a *horse.*"

"A horse?" The smith scanned Todd's face, his suit, and his hands, once more. With a twisted smirk, he said, "More spirited than this, you mean?"

The question was a challenge. Todd had accepted stronger challenges in the past, challenges that could have killed him. One that damn near had. But he no longer felt so invulnerable as he had in the past. He knew now that he could make mistakes. He could fail, lose, even die. He'd be a fool to let his pride get him a broken neck.

Still, he had been a horseman once. He had taken long-boned, hot-headed Irish hunters over fences that had stopped other men. He had mastered balkers, bolters, rearers, horses that tried to scrape him off against every tree, horses that had tried to be rid of him by rolling on him. And even if that had been a long time before, he had ridden recently. Before he left New York, he had spent hours on hired hacks, firming riding muscles, relearning old skills. Most of those had been spoiled horses, hard-headed and hard-mouthed.

And the smith's eyes were so damned insulting.

"Yes," Todd said. "Something more spirited."

The horse the smith brought him this time was a well-built short-coupled young bay gelding. It was smaller than the eastern horses Todd was accustomed to, but handsome in its own way, and wide between the eyes.

"I can promise you this one ain't ruint yet," the smith said.

So it was a green horse, only partially trained, perhaps a bucker. Todd's experience with bucking horses was limited. They weren't so common in Europe or the East.

Wondering if he might be making a serious mistake, he lifted a stirrup to check the girth.

The western saddle was new to him, but he could see how it functioned. There were two cinches, lashed with straps. Both were pulled up firm, but not tight enough.

The smith watched with interest as Todd jammed a knee into the bay's side and jerked up each latigo, then measured the stirrups to his arm and adjusted them. His expression was curious when Todd took the reins and, holding them short, stepped up to the saddle.

Tight on the bit, the bay couldn't get its head down to buck as Todd mounted. Instead, it reared.

Todd felt the fear in the horse, and knew it might fling itself over backwards. But he had ridden such horses before. Even without the off stirrup, he had seat enough to use his weight. Easing rein slightly, he threw himself forward enough to change the horse's point of balance.

For an instant, the horse danced on its hind legs. Then it came down. Shaking its head, it tried to get the reins away from Todd. He answered each jerk with a flex of his hand, at the same time finding the off stirrup and securing his seat.

Suddenly the horse began to whirl. Todd slammed a heel into its flank. He wished he had spurs of some kind, preferably those huge-roweled ones the cowboys fancied. Working heels and reins, he straightened the bay. The spin became a lunge.

The horse decided to run out from under its rider. Frantically, it bolted. But Todd was steady in the big saddle, and the high cantle and pommel helped him stay that way.

The horse was heading uproad, out of town, into the open. Easing rein, Todd let it run. When he felt its wild drive waning, he urged it on. He kept it running until it was moving at his will and not its own. He pushed it until its sides heaved and its stride faltered.

When he shifted his weight back and lightly drew rein, the horse obeyed. Gently keeping it close on the bit, he swung it around. It was at a lope now. He worked it into a trot and discovered that the big saddle was awkward for posting. After a moment, he returned the horse to a lope, then played the reins, collecting the lope into a canter.

It wasn't a bad horse. Not nearly as green as he had feared. The smith hadn't meant for him to break his neck, but just to be shaken up.

And the battle with the horse had been exhilarating. Todd

felt very alive now, rather pleased with himself. But he stifled his smile as he approached the smith.

The smith's eyes allowed him an unwilling respect. Drawing rein, Todd patted the horse's lathered withers. His expression aloof, he told the smith, "An adequate animal."

Then he put the bay into a collected canter again, and rode the length of the main street before he headed for the road that should take him to the Indian spring and, eventually, to Amos McRae.

When he reached the crest of the slope behind the town, Todd discovered a breeze. It was small, but very welcome. Halting, he wiped at the sweat on his face and looked out at the land ahead.

It was broken, rolling land, partly forested, partly brush and dry, brown grass cut with gullies. He could spot a few houses scattered in the distance, and a few cattle browsing where there was shade. To either side, the horizon was jagged. To the left, the peaks were hazy and distant. To the right, they were very sharp and very near. That would be the badlands Edmund had mentioned. The road stretched into the basin ahead, disappearing into a stand of cottonwood.

Following it, Todd found the bridge over the gully Edmund described. The gully itself was a good ten feet deep, its sides shelved, marking different water levels. At the moment, the creek was only a small stream flowing sluggishly along the very bottom of the gully.

Even so, it was water, wet and inviting.

There was a hoof path down the bank of the gully a short distance from the bridge. Todd reined the bay down the path. At the bottom, he dismounted, stretched, and sighed. The bay nosed into the water. Upstream a few paces, Todd squatted and dipped a hand into the creek. He scooped up enough water to slake his thirst, then splashed hands full of it into his face.

It was appreciably cooler in the gully than it had been above. As far as Todd could see, the broad bottom offered enough footing for a horse. He was supposed to follow the creek. He could see no reason not to use the stream bed as a road.

Holding the reins short, he carefully remounted. But the bay'd had its run. It no longer felt like making trouble. After some token snorting and head-tossing, it settled to his commands. At a leisurely walk, he moved it upstream.

By the time he had rounded the first distinct bend, he was certain he was being followed.

He could think of reasons he might be tracked. His appearance could have caught the attention of a thief who meant to waylay him. Someone curious about the stranger in town might have decided to find out where he was headed. Or it might even be a youngster on horseback playing Indian.

There were a few rough spots in the gully that would have been rapids if the stream had been running full and fast. He came to one that was so rough he had to dismount and lead the horse over it. Around the next bend, he halted and dismounted again.

There was a pistol in his pocket, a Remington revolver that held five .32-caliber shots. It was an old gun with a limited range and uncertain accuracy. As he worked it out of the pocket, he wondered if it would be adequate. But he had no intention of using it, unless he was forced to.

Holding the reins in one hand and the gun in the other, he worked back around the bend until he could glimpse the rough stretch. He watched as a horseman appeared.

Suddenly he grinned.

The little man on the big black stallion was Don Edmund.

Edmund looked as heat-drenched in his stiff collar and buttoned suit as Todd felt. Todd thought the man was a fool not to accept local custom and dress for the weather. But he understood that Edmund had a pretense to keep up, too. In his own way, Don Edmund was as unreal as James R. Todd of Richmond, Virginia. An imitation gentleman who depended on dress and manner to maintain the illusion. But there was a difference. Edmund was deluding himself as well as others.

Sliding out of the saddle, Edmund began to pick his way up the rocks. His horse balked and he cursed it. He was suffering for the story he pursued. Well, he would get a story worth suffering for, but not here and now. If everything went according to plan, he wouldn't get it until Todd was far away.

There was no harm in letting Edmund follow now.

Returning the gun to his pocket, Todd mounted up and rode on at a lope. But soon he had to slow to a walk again. The gully bottom was growing rougher and rockier, the footing poorer. Then he found himself facing a boulder-and-mud dam that completely blocked the way. Amos McRae's dam, he supposed. That would mean he was on Pitchfork land now. He caught himself another drink from the water that spilled over the dam, then looked for a way out of the gully.

At the dam the walls were steep. He had to backtrack a few paces to find a slope the horse could climb. As he rode up it, he glimpsed Edmund again. Edmund had yielded to the heat and peeled his coat. He was riding in his shirtsleeves, looking weary and worn. Todd wondered how long he would persist. He seemed to be a dogged little devil.

Reaching the top of the bank, Todd found he was no longer in rolling grassland. Now he was surrounded by an arid litter of sand and stone broken by jagged upthrusts of rock. A few patches of parched, brown weeds struggled to keep life among the rocks. The only true green was the rim of grass edging the pool behind the dam, a narrow, hopeful bit of life in a dead land.

It was a gaunt, somber, oddly awesome land, unlike anything Todd had ever seen before. The harsh spires of stone were fantasies, turrets and battlements of demon castles haunted by the restless spirits of prediluvian sinners. He could see the rock Edmund had called The Squaw. It looked rather like an eroded chess queen, ragged but still regal. The stony mistress of this little piece of hell.

Suddenly lead spanged into the sand ahead of Todd's horse. The sound of a rifle shot slammed against the stone battlements, bounding and rebounding, becoming the mocking laughter of the devils that dwelt there.

Todd's horse snorted. And bolted.

The first shot hadn't been aimed at Todd. The second one was. He sensed the nearness of the slug whining past his head.

The horse was running frantically. Todd wasn't sure whether to urge it on and duck for cover among the rocks, or haul up short and hope the whole thing was a mistake he could explain away.

Before he could decide, he felt the horse jerk under him. It was stumbling. Going down, head over heels. Kicking free of the stirrups, he jumped.

The deep saddle was easy to stay in but hard to get out of. He was off balance as he flung himself from it. He fell awkwardly, spread-eagled, and hit the ground face down with a shock that slammed the breath out of him. It almost stunned him. He lay gasping, momentarily unable to move.

Finally he caught breath and got an arm braced on the ground. Shoving, he rolled over to sit up. And saw a man towering in front of him. A tall, lean young man in rough range clothes, with a broad-brimmed hat pushed to the back of his head and a rifle in his hands. The rifle was pointed directly at Todd's chest.

"Who are you?" the man asked.

The bad fall had rattled Todd. He felt hazy and uncertain. Giving a shake of his head to clear it, he muttered, "James R. Todd of Richmond, Virginia."

The name apparently meant nothing to the man with the gun. "You're a long ways from your own range, mister. What the hell you doing out here?"

"Riding." Todd wondered where Don Edmund was. If this was a real danger, the newspaperman damned well should step in and give a hand. But perhaps it wasn't any real danger and Edmund was watching from hiding, enjoying the show.

Sarcastically, the man with the gun said, "You just happened to be riding down in the gully at the dam?"

"Yes." Todd eyed the rifle, resenting it. He resented the man's attitude. He didn't think he like these damned disrespectful Westerners at all. But he was in no position to say so.

"If that's so, why'd you run when I fired that warning shot at you?" the man asked.

"My horse bolted," Todd said.

The man laughed. "And you fell off!"

Todd caught at a surge of anger and swallowed it back with a sigh. The rifle no longer threatened him. Its muzzle had drooped away from his chest. He got to his feet and wiped at the sand on his suit. Picking up his hat, he brushed the brim. As he set the hat on his head, he took a good look at the man in front of him.

He appeared to be in his early twenties. His face was sun-darkened and weathered but still boyish. A full, ragged mustache the color of the badland sand didn't quite hide the softness of his mouth. Squint lines forming at his eyes suggested quick laughter, but at the moment the amusement in his face was scornful.

His hat and boots were battered but obviously expensive. So was the wide leather belt that held a holstered revolver at his hip. The rest of his clothing was ordinary. The breeches were canvas, the shirt was calico, and the vest drab. All were softened and faded by wear and lye-soap washings. The hands that held the rifle were brown and work-scarred.

It was hard to judge him. At first glance, he might be taken for a common laborer. A manure shoveler or the like. But his attitude was wrong. It went with the expensive hat and boots.

Collecting himself, playing the role of the indignant gentleman, Todd said, "And who are you, sir? By what right dare you shoot at me?"

"This is my land you're trespassing on, mister."

"This is Pitchfork land, isn't it?"

"Yeah."

Todd shook his head. "You aren't Amos McRae."

"I'm his son, Cole. My Pa know you?"

"No."

"I reckon he ought to," Cole said. He gestured with the rifle. "Come on, mister. I think Pa'd be right interested in having a look at you."

CHAPTER 4

Todd's mount was gone, probably well on its way back home, so they rode double on Cole McRae's horse. Todd sat behind the saddle, with the horse's sweat soaking into his trousers. That was bad. The suit would stink of the horse. It would be hard to appear a gentleman when he smelled like a stable.

He wondered how long it would take to get this business over with and get back to civilization.

The trail Cole rode took them out of the badlands into the dry, brown grass and onto a road that Todd guessed was the same one he had left at the bridge. After they had been on it awhile, Todd decided Don Edmund wasn't following them. He wondered if Edmund had seen enough to satisfy him, or had just worn out and given up. Maybe the sight of Cole McRae with a gun had scared him off.

The road meandered across fields and through small woods, then under a crosstree. A whitewashed hayfork hanging from the crosstree announced that this was the gate to the Pitchfork ranch. The wheel ruts ran on under it to swing around a windbreak of pines. Past the pines, Todd saw the ranch buildings.

A medium-sized two-story house sat on a small knoll amid a scattering of cottonwoods. The lower story was of fieldstone. The upper, possibly a later addition, was plank, painted white and trimmed with green woodwork.

A roofed veranda reached by four steps ran the width of the first floor. The door was precisely in the middle, flanked by pairs of curtained windows. A massive stone chimney reared from the center of the hipped roof, New England style. Behind the house, from an attached kitchen, a smaller chimney eased a thin twist of smoke into the clear blue brilliance of the sky.

A wagon barn of fieldstone, and a white-painted, green-trimmed, plank stable were within convenient walking distance of the house.

Walkways from the house were bordered with rocks. Flower beds fronted the veranda. The flowers in them drooped under the glaring sun, but they showed careful tending and regular watering. It was a home that declared a caring woman within.

The working buildings of the ranch, the bunkhouse, cookshack, outbuildings, and stock corrals, were all a good half mile distant. They, too, were whitewashed and well kept, but there were no posies around them.

It was a ranch that looked prosperous, and hopeful of the future.

As they neared the house, Todd caught the scent of baking bread. He realized that he was hungry. Very hungry, and very tired. And dirty. Sweat-soaked, dust-caked, stinking dirty. That was bad. Maybe he should have hired that rig the blacksmith recommended and driven directly to the door, looking like the gentleman of affluence he was supposed to be.

But that way he would have been making the first move himself. This way, he was being forced to meet Amos McRae. With luck, he would be similarly forced to give a reason for riding out to the Indian spring. Forced, apparently against his will, into confiding in McRae.

The door opened as Cole drew rein in front of the house. The man who came out onto the veranda had to be Amos McRae. His face was Cole's with something like thirty years added. They were years that had made it harder and wiser, and erased any trace of boyishness. The weathered creases were deep and the sandy mustache was streaked with gray. But the jaw line, the nose, the eyes, were the same. His clothes, too, were like Cole's, though they looked freshly laundered, and he wore no hat or gun.

As he walked onto the veranda, he limped heavily, favoring

his right leg. He came to the head of the steps and leaned a shoulder against a roof support. Squinting at Todd, he called, "What's this?"

Todd slid down off the horse's rump. His thigh joints were stiffening from so much riding in one morning, and his shoulders ached. Under his hat, his hair was soaking. Sweat trickled from his brows and down his cheeks into his beard. His attire was dirty and rumpled, and the scent of the horse clung to him.

Mustering more genteel dignity than he felt, he bowed slightly to Amos McRae. "James R. Todd, sir, at your service."

The elder McRae looked him down, then looked in question at Cole.

"I caught him messing around the dam," Cole said.

"I happened to be riding past your dam when your son stopped me and insisted I see you," Todd told Amos.

"Happened to be riding past the dam?" Amos said. "Where's your horse?"

Cole answered, "I took a shot to warn him, and he tried to light out, only he fell off his horse and it got away from him. I didn't figure his poor, tender feet could take him far, so I give him a ride."

Resentful of the implication that he had toppled off the horse like some damned duffer, Todd said, "I was hardly *lighting out*. I had hired a rather green mount. It bolted at the gunshot and fell with me."

Cole snorted.

A woman appeared in the doorway behind Amos. Coming onto the veranda, she asked, "What is it, Pa?"

"Cole found a stray on our range," Amos told her.

She was a McRae, too. It showed in her face and her stance. Amos's daughter, Asia, no doubt. She was a little younger than Cole, perhaps nineteen or twenty. Her sandy hair was drawn back severely, and her clothes were harshly simple. A plain brown riding skirt held by a broad leather belt, and a faded green print calico shirtwaist open at the throat. The hem of the skirt came only to her ankles. It showed scuffed sharp-toed riding boots such as the men wore.

She looked boyish, plain, fashionless, a common country girl who would grow fat and ugly with too much childbearing, or gaunt and ugly with too much hard work. A disappointingly dull creature. Todd had hoped McRae's daughter might add spice to his job.

Giving her a polite bit of a bow, he introduced himself.

She didn't answer, but eyed him, her gaze openly appraising and far too bold. Very improper. And oddly embarrassing.

"I found him messing around the dam," Cole told her.

She addressed Todd then. "What were you doing at the dam?"

"Riding past," he intoned, making it clear he had answered that question more than once already and was weary of it. "I was on my way to visit an Indian spring I understand is in the vicinity. I had been directed to follow Stick Creek. Inevitably I passed your dam. Had I known my presence there would cause such distress, I would have gladly gone far out of my way to avoid it."

Asia smiled as if she found him rather amusing.

Amos asked, "Who directed you that way?"

"A gentleman at the newspaper office."

"Edmund?" Cole snapped.

"I believe that was his name," Todd said. "Now, if you don't mind, I have had a tiring morning. I would like to return to town. As Mr. McRae's rash gunfire has lost me my mount, I would appreciate it if you would permit me to rent an animal from your stable. I assure you, I will arrange for its return as quickly as possible."

Amos harrumphed and said, "Couldn't hardly do that, Mr. Todd. It wouldn't be right to take money off you for the lend of a horse if you're just what you claim to be. Wouldn't be smart to let you go running off loose if you ain't."

"What would I be but what I say I am?" Todd said stiffly.

Amos shrugged. "Suppose you come on inside where we can set comfortable, and you explain to me what you wanted to see the Indian spring for."

Asia led Todd into the house through a small entry hall and into a sitting room. Amos and Cole followed.

The parlor was square, with windows spilling sunlight in on two sides. The sofa, chairs, and small tables were in the popular mission style, severely simple in themselves, but their basic simplicity was overridden by a fashionable clutter of lambrequins and knickknacks. There was a good Brussels carpet on the floor, and a looming Gothic parlor organ in one corner. It wasn't much different from middle-class parlors the nation over. It suggested more concern with the niceties of civilization than Todd had anticipated in this wilderness.

As Todd entered through one door, a woman came into the parlor through another. She smiled at Todd as if he were an invited guest. Her smile was open and hospitable with none of the underlying suspicion he had seen in the faces of the others.

She was a small-boned, plump woman of around fifty, with a face that showed a resemblance to Asia but none at all to Amos. Todd supposed she was Amos's wife, Sarah. She was undoubtedly the one who tended the flower beds. She had the look of a very contented cook and housewife about her. Her gray hair was neatly pinned with tortoise-shell combs. Her dress was a simple gingham frock with enough frills and flounces to suggest a definite interest in popular styles. Probably a copy of something out of Godey's.

"Amos," she said brightly, "I didn't know we were expecting a caller."

"Didn't expect him," Amos answered. "He just sort of happened along."

"Won't you introduce him?"

"Sarah, this here is Mr. Todd. Todd, this is my missus, Sarah."

Todd accepted her hand in the Continental manner. She blushed, almost tittering, as he pressed his lips to it. And he knew that, whatever followed, she would be on his side.

Amos introduced Asia then. But when Todd kissed her hand, her reaction was more amused than impressed.

Amos extended his own hand. Todd gave it the kind of firm, forthright shake that claimed he had nothing to hide from anyone. It was a handshake Todd had studied and practiced until it came naturally.

Cole shook hands reluctantly, with obvious distaste. Whatever followed, he certainly would not be on Todd's side.

With the formalities done, they seated themselves. Todd sank wearily into a deep-cushioned armchair. He wasn't in the mood for this. He would sooner have settled into a warm bath, then a soft bed. But money for baths and beds had to come from somewhere. Concentrating on the role he played, he waited for someone else to open the conversation.

Sarah McRae did it eagerly. She perched on the edge of the chair facing him, happy excitement at having a new guest glittering in her eyes. "What brings you to Pitchfork, Mr. Todd?"

He gave her a wry, rueful smile as he said, "Brute force, madame. Your son brought me here at gun point."

"Oh!" She darted Cole a disapproving scowl.

Amos came to his son's defense. "Cole caught him messing around the dam."

"I was *passing* the dam," Todd said, addressing Sarah. "I was simply riding by on my way to an Indian spring I understand is in the vicinity."

"What would you want to go up to that old place for?" Sarah asked.

"That," Asia said, "is the question."

"I wanted to see it. Is that a crime?"

"*Why* did you want to see it?"

"Why not? Is it so unusual for a traveler to want to visit a local point of interest?"

Amos said, "Not many folks would think that old spring is a point of interest."

"It happens that I do," Todd said.

"Why?" Asia asked.

Todd sighed. As if he'd had enough of their questioning, he said, "Perhaps I was mistaken."

"Amos," Sarah said suddenly. "When Johnny brought in the firewood this morning, he told me there was talk at the bunkhouse about a stranger in town looking to buy up a lot of land."

Amos lifted a brow at Todd. "You wouldn't happen to be that same stranger, would you?"

"I have never said I was interested in buying up land," Todd said.

"That don't exactly answer my question."

"I have no idea whether I am the same stranger. I do not know how many strangers might happen to be in town at the moment, or what their business might be."

"But you do know what I mean. Just what is *your* business in town, Mr. Todd?"

Todd felt like giving a direct answer and getting all this over with quickly. But it wouldn't look good if he surrendered too easily. He kept stalling with evasions a while longer. At last he admitted, "I wanted to have a good look at the spring. If it's what I understand it to be, I thought I might offer to buy it."

"Why?" Asia asked.

Todd made a point of not quite meeting her eyes. "I thought I might like to build there."

"Build what?"

"A sort of lodge."

"What kind of lodge?" Cole snapped at him.

Todd let himself look flustered, badgered beyond the limits of his patience. Taking a deep breath, he addressed Amos. "Sir, I intended to make a simple examination of the property and, if it suited my purposes, to make you a fair offer for it. But if you insist on trying to hold me up for an exorbitant price, I will go elsewhere."

"What the goddamned hell are you talking about?" Amos grunted.

"Pa!" Sarah was taken aback at his language. Her eyes reproached him for it.

He gave her a look of embarrassed apology, then glared

defiantly at his children. Asia and Cole exchanged glances of
silent amusement. Evidently Amos's lapses into strong language were a recurring problem to their mother.

With a harrumph, Amos turned to Todd again. "You'd better explain what you mean, mister. What is it about that old
spring that might make me ask an exorbitant price for it?"

"Nothing!" Todd rose to his feet. "Sir, I am no longer interested in buying your property at any price. I do not even
care to see it. I wish only to return to town and take the next
coach back to civilization. If you please, I will need some
form of transportation—"

"Mr. Todd!" Sarah protested. She turned to Amos. "Pa,
can't you see the poor man is worn out? You've been brow-
beating him as if he were a horsethief or something. What
will he think of us out here?"

"A man comes sneaking around like a fox eying a henhouse
and then won't admit what he's up to, he can figure on what
he'll get," Amos grumbled.

Cole nodded vigorously in agreement.

"Pa has a point," Asia said, her bold eyes on Todd. "You
have been furtive and evasive, Mr. Todd. I think we have a
right to know just why you're so interested in our spring."

"You stop that!" Sarah told her daughter. "You let the
poor man catch his breath. Mr. Todd, it's getting on to dinnertime. We'd be pleased if you'd stay and eat with us."

"Thank you, madame, but I fear your hospitality is not
shared."

"It is!" she insisted. She turned to her family and demanded, "He is welcome, isn't he? Tell him. Tell him you're
all ashamed of the way you've been acting."

Amos sighed. "Mr. Todd, maybe we have been rough on
you. But it looks like there's trouble making around these
parts, and we're all kind of spooky about it. And it does seem
downright strange you'd go riding up to the spring alone without so much as you even talked to me about it first."

"Perhaps," Todd admitted wearily. "Possibly I was in error
trespassing on your property. If so, I regret it. I would rather

none of this had occurred. I think it best I leave now and we forget the matter entirely."

"But you did trespass," Asia said. "Now you owe us an explanation."

"I think not," Todd answered. "If you please, about a horse—"

Sarah interrupted. "Won't you please stay for dinner, Mr. Todd? We hardly ever get any visitors from back East. There's so much I'd like to talk to you about. If we promise not to ask any more questions about that old spring and your personal business, will you stay?"

Todd couldn't keep on trying to leave. They might give in and let him go. He smiled at Sarah. "You are a most gracious lady. I really would appreciate the opportunity to rest awhile."

She returned his smile with happy relief, then spoke to her family. "Now, nobody is to mention that old spring again. Is that agreed?"

"We won't mention it," Asia conceded, "until after dinner."

Amos nodded.

"I got to take care of my horse," Cole grumbled. He started for the door. "I'll eat at the cookshack."

"Cole!" Sarah protested. But he slammed on out of the house. She shook her head sadly at his lack of manners. Then she smiled at Todd again. "If you'll excuse me, I have some chores in the kitchen. Asia, come give me a hand."

Asia's gaze lingered a moment longer on Todd. Then she followed her mother out of the parlor.

Todd reseated himself, leaning back in the chair, enjoying the long moment of silence that he knew Amos was finding awkward.

Amos finally figured out something to say. "You like a drink, Mr. Todd?"

Todd thought he'd like a lot of them. A whole damned bottle. He said, "Thank you, I would."

"I got corn whiskey and brandywine and some berry wines Ma put up herself."

It would have been politic to try Sarah McRae's homemade wine, but she seemed the type who would make very mild drink. Todd wanted something he could feel. "The brandy, if you please."

Amos got the bottle out of a cupboard and poured for himself and Todd. It was an adequate brandy. Todd savored it. Soon he began to feel the relaxing warmth of it. Very nice.

Go easy, Todd warned himself. The worst was yet to come, and he had to be alert for it.

Amos made a stab at conversation. "You staying in town, Mr. Todd?"

"Yes. At the hotel."

"Been in town long?"

"I arrived yesterday."

"What do you think of Stick City?"

The brandy wanted to tell the truth. Todd didn't dare let it. He compromised. "It's quite a bit different from Richmond, Virginia."

Amos chuckled. "Maybe it ain't much now, but it will be, once we get the railroad in."

Startled, Todd tensed. He asked, "Are you expecting the railroad to build in?"

"One of these days we'll get them here," Amos said with a sigh. "They got to come someday."

Todd hid his relief behind the brandy glass. Amos was only hopeful. He knew nothing. Todd asked him, "You'd like to see the railroad come in?"

"I damn sure would. It would mean a lot to us cattlemen."

They went on talking, discussing the town and the ranches around it. When Todd's glass was empty, Amos filled it again. Todd noticed that he only topped off his own, half-full glass. It occurred to Todd that Amos was trying to oil his tongue with brandy.

He was smiling inwardly, certain the day would be a success, when Sarah called them to wash up for dinner.

CHAPTER 5

Sarah had changed her house frock for a summer gown. A Sunday churchgoing dress from the look of it. She had added bits of jewelry. Too many bits. But she didn't know that. Her eyes sparkled with pride and her cheeks were rosy with excitement when she called the men in to dinner.

Her appearance amused Todd. He felt pleasantly flattered by the trouble she had gone to for his visit. She had dressed the dining table as well as herself. It was a large, round table perched on a pedestal. The damask cloth she had spread over it smelled of camphor and cedar, betraying that it was kept stored in a chest awaiting occasions important enough to warrant its use. The Fenton porcelain place settings probably came out only for such occasions, too.

But Asia had done nothing in honor of his visit. She came to the table still wearing the same appallingly plain clothing she'd had on when Todd arrived. She hadn't so much as pinched color into her cheeks. Todd found himself oddly disappointed by her lack of concern about the impression she made on him.

He told himself she knew she was plain, knew nothing could disguise that plainness. But he would have appreciated her caring enough to try. He wondered in passing why he should care. But there was no time to think about it. He had business to attend.

Once the grace had been said and the plates were filled, Todd took control of the conversation, aiming it at Sarah. The attention delighted her. Soon he had her talking about herself, at ease and speaking freely, loving every moment of it.

She told him how she'd been born in Vermont, the daugh-

ter of a small shopkeeper, how the family had moved West
when she was in her teens, how much she had disliked making the move until she met Amos McRae. She spoke tenderly
of meeting Amos, of a shockingly quick courtship, and of an
elopement that had horrified her parents. Her every word and
gesture told Todd that she loved her husband and her children and her home in the West. But there was a wistfulness
in her as she reminisced about the small elegances of her middle-class childhood in the East.

Suddenly, to Asia's obvious embarrassment, Sarah was
confiding in Todd about her daughter. Sarah had hoped to
rear Asia to the social graces. She had pestered Amos into letting her send the girl East to a proper ladies' academy. But
after one season, Asia had refused to go back. Asia was too re-
bellious, too much her father's child. Sadly, Sarah admitted
she simply couldn't do a thing with the girl.

But as Sarah spoke of her disappointment with her daughter, Todd could sense a pride, too. An admiration, as if Sarah
secretly envied the girl she couldn't fully understand.

As he ate, Todd glanced curiously at Asia, and he realized
he didn't understand her either. She was very unlike the
women he had known in society. He understood the ones like
himself, the ones hiding behind masks, playing roles. He understood the cat-clawed, green-eyed gossips; the languid, limp-
eyed romantics; the sharp-eyed intriguers, all involved with
manipulating the people around them, all jockeying for social
position, for romantic conquests, for power. He had them cat-
egorized. He could anticipate them, use their patterns and
weaknesses to his own ends. But he couldn't fit Asia into the
patterns he was familiar with.

Not yet, he told himself. But he would find her pattern,
and learn the ways to make use of it, just as he had already
done with her mother.

Glancing at her, he discovered her eyes were hazel. Clear
and bright eyes like gemstones. Remarkably pretty eyes for
such a plain face. Sparkling eyes filled with a joy of living.

Eyes with a quality to them that he didn't recognize at all. They puzzled him.

He found he had to concentrate to keep his mind on the conversation with Sarah. His attention kept wanting to drift back to the enigma of Asia McRae.

Amos took small part in the conversation. He kept his promise not to question Todd during the dinner, but his thoughts were obviously filled with questions. He kept gazing at Todd, appraising him, wondering about him.

When the meal was done, Amos led Todd back into the parlor and offered him another drink and a cigar. Todd accepted and settled into the easy chair again. Amos sat down across from him and began to talk. He didn't ask questions yet. He rambled on about the cattle business.

Todd downed his brandy. He could feel the liquor working in him. The feeling was very pleasant. Very tempting.

Amos refilled the glass, then returned to the subject of cattle. Todd understood that Amos was stalling, hoping the brandy would weaken Todd's defenses, before he began asking the questions that danced behind his eyes.

But Todd knew his capacity. He knew the small voice in the back of his mind that would stay sober long after his hands began to shake and his tongue thicken and his knees refuse to hold his weight. He knew from experience just how much it took to drown that voice. He knew he was capable of drinking a lot more than he intended to put away here and now.

Amos McRae didn't know. Amos would believe what he saw. He would believe the way Todd leaned back, appearing relaxed, very at ease, just drunk enough to confide in a stranger, perhaps let his tongue slip its tether.

Amos was on his feet, filling Todd's glass for the third time, when Asia and Sarah came into the parlor. Todd rose, his movements loose but not uncontrolled. He saw the ladies seated, then settled into the armchair again and sipped at the brandy.

Sarah wasn't interested in talking about the cattle business.

The questions she wanted to ask weren't the ones Amos had in mind. She wanted to know about Todd himself, and about life back East.

He had his answers ready for her. Before he arrived in Stick City, he had composed a biography for the character he played. He told her he had traveled extensively in Europe in past years but of late had been too involved in business affairs to enjoy much social life.

She commiserated with him. Then, trying to be delicate about it, she asked after his family. Her delicacy was heavy-handed. He recognized her intent. She was considering him as a possible match for her daughter.

"I'm afraid I have never had time for the pleasures of courtship and marriage," he said, glancing covertly at Asia.

He saw the faintest suggestion of color rise to her cheeks. That was interesting. He wondered if it would serve his purpose to play the game. She might be plain, but she wasn't really unattractive. Not exactly.

She caught his glance. Her eyes darted away an instant. Then they met his with that disconcerting overboldness. Lovely hazel eyes.

Abruptly she interrupted her mother to say, "And now, Mr. Todd, maybe you'd like to tell us why you're so interested in the Indian spring?"

Her gaze was a challenge. She offered him a battle of wills. He knew that to win he should lose. It was a thing he had done often enough in the past. It was part of his technique to pretend he had been overpowered by the will of the person he was maneuvering. Knowing his own strength, his own position, he had never been bothered by the pretense of weakness. Now, though, he found himself curiously unwilling to yield. He felt as if it actually were a battle of wills instead of a game of trickery.

He told himself he was losing his touch. Slipping. That was bad. He had to carry this game through. He had to win it. This was his last chance.

"You really do owe us some explanation, you know," Asia was saying.

He realized she was back-stepping. She was easing the pressure of her will against him. She was willing to ask instead of demand. That was good. It made it easier for him to give in. He said, "I suppose I do."

She broke the gaze then, looking toward her father.

Todd turned to Amos. "You've heard of Saratoga Springs in New York? White Sulphur Springs in Virginia?"

Amos nodded.

"They are very successful health resorts," Todd went on. "As successful as the spas of Europe. Wealthy Americans are coming to prefer the luxuries of their own country to the decadence of Europe. In the East, people are looking westward. They are becoming very conscious of the new land out here. They want to see Pike's Peak and the Yellowstone. They are interested in the western states and territories. And I am interested in developing a resort, a genuinely American spa, here in the West for them. *If* I can find a suitable mineral spring to build it around."

"Our spring?" Asia asked.

"Amos!" Sarah gasped, beaming with excitement. "We'll absolutely have to get new wallpaper for the parlor and new music lamps for the organ! I don't know what I'll do for something to wear! I'll need help sewing! Asia—oh, goodness —Asia, you'll simply *have* to do something about that horrible suntan! Rosewater and tincture of benzoin might help. And lemon juice. And a bonnet. That terrible hat you wear just isn't sufficient, and—"

"Hold on, Ma," Amos interrupted, waving a hand at her. "Nobody's coming yet."

She looked as if he had thrown a bucket of water at her. Her face sagged in disappointment. Then slowly, hopefully, she asked, "They *will* come, won't they?"

Amos hesitated. His voice was gentle with sympathy for her. "I'm sorry, Ma, but it ain't likely."

She turned to Todd for assurance.

"I haven't seen your spring yet," he answered her. "I have no idea whether it would be suitable or not."

Amos resented the hope Todd offered her. He snapped, "It wouldn't, and you know it."

Todd looked blankly at him. "What do you mean?"

"You know damn well we're too far from the railroad here. You've found out for yourself what a rough trip it is here by stagecoach. You don't really believe a lot of rich eastern folk would take all that hard traveling just to get out here to a spring when there's a lot of other good springs right close to the railroad. Or are you trying to sell us some kind of poke that ain't really got a pig in it at all, Mr. Todd?"

That was too close to the truth. For an instant, Todd was flustered. He covered by taking a long sip of the brandy he held. The liquor was warm in his veins. He glared at Amos, reassuming the air of insulted dignity he had played earlier. It was an air of anger, tinged now with brandy heat. An attitude that might make a man let slip things he hadn't meant to say.

Rising, he said, "I am not trying to sell you anything, sir. I *had* thought I might buy land from you, but I wouldn't have your spring now as a gift. There certainly must be other springs adequate to my purposes, and people less reluctant to benefit from the resort and the railroad that would connect with it."

"*Railroad!*" Asia pounced on the word.

As if he hadn't heard her, Todd went on speaking, now addressing Sarah. "Mrs. McRae, I appreciate your hospitality, but—"

"Hold on!" Amos snapped. "What about a railroad?"

Todd hesitated. He still held the brandy glass. He looked at it as if it had betrayed him. "Did I say railroad?"

"You did."

This was a critical point. Todd weighed each tone of voice, each flicker of facial expression. Slowly he said, "I suppose it— well, it hardly matters now. You can't press me for some outrageous price if I'm not buying the land."

"*What* about the railroad?" Amos insisted.

Todd met his eyes. "I expect a branch line to be built into the area where I construct my spa."

Amos almost flinched. A railroad into Stick City would mean far more to him than just an influx of tourists. It would mean an end to the long, hard trail drives that endangered men and melted salable meat off the cattle. An end to drives like the one that had cost him a son.

Wary of his own sudden hopes, he said, "What gives you that notion, Mr. Todd?"

"It has been arranged."

"How do you mean?"

"I'm not at liberty to discuss it, sir."

"Look here, Todd!" Amos exploded. "If you—!"

"Pa!" Sarah shouted. "You stop that! You stop bullying poor Mr. Todd!"

Amos glared at her for an instant. Then he eased back. His voice caught in his throat. "I'm sorry, Mr. Todd, but the truth is, we *need* a railroad in these parts. We need one bad. If you got a way to bring us one, I'd sure as hell like to know about it."

Asia stood taut, watching Todd, searching his face.

Todd took a deep breath as if he struggled with his own temper. Coldly, he said, "There is no point in our discussing it, sir. The matter is now closed."

"Does it have to be?" Asia said. "Can't we forget this petty quarreling and start over again at the beginning?"

"Petty quarreling?" Todd looked taken aback at the phrase.

Calmly, reasonably, Asia said, "That's what it is, isn't it?"

He hesitated, giving it a thoughtful moment, then relented. "Perhaps you're right. This has been an exceedingly difficult day. I am not at all myself at the moment."

"At the moment, we're all under a strain, Mr. Todd," she said. "Here in Stick City, we're suffering a drought that may ruin some of the ranchers. Tempers are short. The newspaper has been running some very unpleasant editorials and people are upset. There could be serious trouble. We are all under a strain."

Amos nodded in agreement. "We need rain bad. And we need a railroad bad. If you can help us, Mr. Todd, we'd be obliged if you'd forget our differences and tell us just what you got in mind."

"Perhaps," Todd muttered thoughtfully. He licked his lips and glanced from one anxious face to another. He sighed as if he had reached a reluctant decision. "This isn't solely my own project. I have a partner—I'd best not mention his name—and I have a responsibility. He proposes to invest sixty thousand dollars in this project. I, myself, intend to supply an additional forty thousand. With the guarantee of our financing, the railroad will—this is all confidential, mind you—strictly *sub rosa*—"

Amos looked at Sarah. Sternly, he said, "That means *secret*, Ma. You don't tell anybody. Not anybody."

"I know," she murmured, watching Todd eagerly.

Todd went on. "The railroad has been contemplating expansion, and will solidify its plans at the next board meeting. I have discussed the matter with certain persons, and I have a firm agreement that if I have completed my negotiations before the board meets, the railroad will definitely route a proposed branch line to serve my spa. You understand, sir, this is all confidential. Unofficial."

Amos nodded.

"There is still the matter of locating a suitable spring for my spa," Todd added.

Sarah said, "Our spring is lovely, Mr. Todd. I know it would do."

Todd gave her a small smile. "I wouldn't know."

"Why don't you plan on going to see the spring in the morning?" Asia suggested. "Pa and I will be glad to show it to you. Won't we, Pa?"

"Sure," Amos answered.

"If you like our spring," Asia told Todd. "We can discuss it then. If you don't like it, there won't be anything to discuss."

"That might be—yes—I think perhaps I should do that," Todd said. "But I must warn you now, no matter how suitable your spring may be, I have already budgeted for land purchase. I do not intend to meet any outrageous price for it."

"I don't intend to ask one," Amos said. "I'm no thief, Mr. Todd. If you want to buy the spring and I decide to sell it to you, it'll be to both our benefit, and I'll set you a price that's fair to both of us."

Todd doubted that. He had never yet known a man who wouldn't milk every possible cent of profit out of a business deal, and then squeeze hard for more. Promises were just so many words, just so much air added to the wind. It was greed that made men rich, and greed that made them gullible. It was Amos McRae's greed for the profit a railroad would bring him that Todd was depending on now.

Todd had shown Amos the bait. It was time to let him contemplate it. Time for Todd to take his leave of the McRaes and let them discuss him behind his back.

CHAPTER 6

The horse that Amos loaned Todd was a dun gelding, a well-mannered animal that stood quietly to be mounted and stepped out briskly when he lifted rein. Its walk was lively, its lope easy. A definite improvement over the bay Todd had hired and lost.

Todd wondered if he would have to pay a price for the lost horse. If he did, he told himself, it would come out of expenses and not his share of the profit.

As he rode toward town, his thoughts drifted. He smiled slightly at the idea of Sarah picking him as a match for her daughter. But his amusement was thin, and vaguely disturbed.

He didn't want to think about Asia.

He didn't want to think at all. He wanted to rest. He felt an urge to get thoroughly drunk. Drunk enough to silence the small voice in his mind. But that was no good. He couldn't get drunk until this affair was over. He couldn't take chances.

But he was so damned tired.

When he left the horse at the livery stable, he learned the bay had been caught and returned. The blacksmith's eyes glittered with pleasure, happy at the idea that the bay had dumped the high and mighty dude. Todd took no offense. He just didn't feel like bothering. From the livery stable, he went directly to his hotel room.

Stripped, he sprawled on the bed. He dozed. Dreamed. And finally woke to find the sky beyond the window a fading twilight violet with flecks of stars already showing in it.

It was probably too late for the hotel dining room, he

thought as he dressed. He had missed supper. And he was hungry.

The lobby was empty when he went downstairs. Nobody to ask about an eating place. He stepped out onto the street and looked at the bright lanterns and glowing windows that marked the town's saloons.

The one next to the hotel lobby was nearest. As good as any, he supposed. He touched his cravat, adjusted the set of his hat, then shoved open a batwing and walked in.

The room was long and narrow, with a bar down one wall and tables lined up along the other. The hanging Rochester lamps were dirty, the light dim and smoky. The sawdust on the floor was scant, matted and muddy where drinks had been spilled. Stuffed heads of wild game hanging behind the bar looked moth-eaten and exhausted, as if their baleful glass eyes had observed too much of life. The whole place stank of stale beer and stale sweat. But at least it was quiet. Only a couple of men stood at the bar. Only a few more bunched at tables.

They all looked toward Todd as he entered. Several whispered together. Most turned their eyes away quickly, making a show of minding their own business.

The lone bartender was a lanky man with eyes like those of the stuffed moose over his head. He gave Todd a meaningless professional smile. "What'll it be, mister?"

"Beer." Todd figured that would appease his appetite if he couldn't find more solid food. Hopefully he asked, "Can you tell me, sir, if it might be possible for a person to obtain a meal at this hour somewhere in town?"

The bartender furrowed his brow into a thoughtful frown. "Tell you what, mister. I live right back of here. Just across the alley. I'm sure my missus could put you together a couple of sandwiches, if that'll do."

Todd supposed it would do.

"You take a table. Set down. I'll have the boy fetch them over as soon as they're ready," the bartender said. He darted to the back door and let out a holler. After a moment, he was back at the bar, giving Todd a smile and a nod.

Todd settled down with his beer to wait. The beer was tepid, but the taste was acceptable. He sipped at it slowly. Eventually a lanky boy with sad, moose eyes came in carrying a plate covered by a ragged napkin. The bartender gave a jerk of his head toward Todd, and the boy delivered the plate to him. There were two thick, altogether decent-looking beef sandwiches on it. Todd nodded approval and gave the boy half a dollar. It was more than the sandwiches and service were worth, but no more than would be expected of him.

The boy delivered the money to his father and left.

The beef was tough but the bread was fresh and Todd was hungry. He began to feel more relaxed as he ate. Until Don Edmund came striding through the batwings.

Edmund didn't hesitate at all. Scanning the room, he fixed on Todd and headed directly toward him. The long, lean compositor with the prominent Adam's apple was close at his heels.

Todd tensed.

"Mr. Todd!" Edmund said heartily, as if he had made a rare and wonderful discovery. "How good to see you again!"

"Mr. Edmund," Todd said, rising to meet him, wishing to hell one or the other of them had gone someplace else. He wished he could ignore the editor or rebuff the intrusion. But it wouldn't have fit the role he played. He smiled.

Edmund indicated the man at his heels. "Mr. Todd, this is my compositor, Andy Groseille. Andy, this is Mr.—ah—James Todd."

"Pleased to meet you," the compositor said, holding out a hand that, despite severe scrubbing, showed the in-ground grime of printer's ink. His eyes were a pale, glassy blue. They peered intently at Todd as Todd accepted the ink-stained hand.

Edmund's eyes glittered. Todd could imagine his nose twitching eagerly at the scent of a story. The hard ride that morning hadn't cooled any of Edmund's fire. He still wore that diabolical look, as if he were on the track of a fresh soul for hell.

He glanced at the empty chairs around the table, obviously wanting to join Todd.

Todd had no choice but to play the game. Forcing any hint of reluctance out of his voice, he invited Edmund and Groseille to sit down.

Edmund seated himself across from Todd, with Groseille at his right. He called for drinks all around, then leaned forward and asked Todd, "How was your morning ride? Did you find the Indian spring?"

Todd was certain Edmund knew everything that had happened that morning, at least up to the point where Cole McRae had hauled him off to the ranch. Now Edmund wanted to know the rest. He was avid to find out what had happened at the ranch.

Todd told him, "No, I encountered one of the McRae family on the way and visited the Pitchfork ranch instead. I dined with the McRaes."

Edmund lifted a brow. To Groseille he said, "Social news. Don't let me forget to include that in the column."

Groseille nodded. His eyes stayed on Todd.

The bartender arrived with their drinks. Edmund sat silent, as if he had been interrupted in the middle of a conspiracy. He didn't speak again until the barkeep was back at his station, well out of earshot. Then he smiled at Todd and continued, "Interesting people, the McRaes. You know that the old man, Amos, founded Stick City?"

"I didn't know," Todd admitted.

"Oh, yes. He came here something like thirty years ago. Sometime before the Civil War. He brought goods to trade with the Indians. He set up a small outpost and started running a few cattle for his own use. But after the war, the cattle business began to prove more profitable than trading, so he ran out the Indians to make room for his herds. Then other ranchers started moving in on him. Now they're cramping him. He wants to run them out and absorb their lands and herds himself."

"You're sure of that?" Todd said.

Edmund smiled. "Certainly. Tell me, Mr. Todd, wouldn't you if you were in his position?"

Of course, Todd thought. But he said, "You have proof?"

"Isn't that dam he built proof enough?"

"It looked like a very small dam to me."

"Oh, yes, and he's got a good story about conserving the water and sharing it with the others. He doesn't want them to realize what he's up to. He doesn't want them banding together against him. He doesn't want a war on his hands. He wants to ease them out gently, before they know what's happening. But believe me, Mr. Todd, there will be trouble around here before this summer is over."

"You'll see to it that there is?" Todd said, and he wondered why he had said it. Antagonizing Edmund was no part of the game.

But Edmund only laughed. "I don't *make* trouble, Mr. Todd. I only report it."

"Of course," Todd said, fighting the skepticism that wanted to sneak into his voice.

"Of course," Edmund echoed cheerfully.

Todd ventured, "You wouldn't object to trouble, if it were to occur here?"

"It would be news. News is my business. Speaking of business, Mr.—ah—Todd, may I ask if you are in Stick City on business, or for pleasure?"

"I think you know already."

"Oh, I hear rumors. Something about making investments. Buying up land. All gossip. There is even some speculation that you're a secret buyer for the railroad, here to pick up right-of-way property as cheaply as possible before word gets out that the land will become valuable."

"Do you believe that?"

"No," Edmund said with a quirky smile.

Todd glanced at Groseille. The compositor sat aloof from the conversation, sipping his drink, gazing at Todd over the rim of the glass.

To Edmund, Todd said, "May I ask what you do believe?"

"That you want something from the McRaes."

"And may I ask what it is that *you* want from the McRaes?"

Edmund's smile weakened. Little hell-fires flashed in his eyes. He touched a fingertip to his mustache, smoothing it down.

Groseille grinned slightly, just for an instant.

Todd thought that whatever it was Edmund wanted from the McRaes, he had already tried for it and had failed to get it. Now he was after revenge. He was attacking the Pitchfork ranch and trying to stir up trouble in retaliation for the failure.

Edmund changed the subject. "Mr. Todd, are you by any chance related to Mrs. Leland Deland of Boston? The former Alice Todd?"

Todd knew Leland Deland and his wife. Once, Todd had helped the Colonel take over thirty thousand dollars from them in a swindle. They had never suspected the truth, but assumed they had made a legitimate business mistake. Their youngest daughter, Ellie, had ticklish knees.

"A very distant relationship at best," he said. "Is she a friend of yours?"

"I worked for Deland once, on that newspaper of his." Edmund sounded bitter. Todd supposed Deland had fired him.

Groseille was still staring. The compositor's gaze crawled over Todd, prodding at every line of his face. Bothered, Todd finally looked directly at him. Caught staring, Groseille turned quickly, guiltily, away.

Feeling wary, Todd asked, "Have we met somewhere before, Mr. Groseille?"

Groseille swallowed. He met Todd's eyes defiantly now. "Do I look familiar?"

Todd shook his head. "Do *I*?"

"Should you?"

Groseille's evasiveness was enough to send small shivers along Todd's spine. But he kept a sociable smile on his face as he said, "You were looking at me as if you thought you might know me from somewhere."

Edmund interrupted. "It seems unlikely that you would travel in the same social circles as a poor newspaper compositor, Mr. Todd."

But a man could be known outside his social circles. And while the things that had happened in Paris were kept out of the papers, they had become current gossip. Todd flicked his tongue across dry lips. He said, "Groseille is an interesting name. French, isn't it?"

The compositor nodded.

"Are you from France?" Todd asked him.

"I was born and raised in Newark, New Jersey."

"Perhaps you have relatives in France?"

"Perhaps."

"Undoubtedly," Edmund put in. "All of us must have relatives of some degree or another in the homelands of our ancestors."

Groseille nodded.

"Lovely country, France," Todd said, speaking to Groseille. "Have you ever been there?"

Edmund interrupted again. "That's Andy's ambition, to go to Paris and study art. He's quite an artist. I mean really talented. He does engravings and woodcuts for the *Sentinel*. He's very good with likenesses. Would you care to have your portrait done, Mr. Todd?"

"You have a good face for it," Groseille said. "A distinctive face. It would be easy to do a likeness of you."

Todd frowned slightly, disliking what Groseille had said. The last thing he wanted was a distinctive face. But perhaps that accounted for Groseille's staring. Perhaps the man simply had an artist's interest in faces as potential subjects.

Edmund was talking. "I've always wanted to travel in Europe myself. At present, however, my small enterprise here takes up all of my time."

"Exhausting business, operating a newspaper," Todd said, thinking of Edmund's ride that morning.

Edmund smiled. Expansively he said, "At times, Mr. Todd, but it's Andy here who does the real work."

"I do my share," Groseille grunted. Evidently he felt that he did more than his share.

Edmund lifted a questioning brow at him.

Groseille gave a very slight nod.

Turning to Todd again, Edmund pushed back his chair and got to his feet. "Well, it's been a pleasure chatting with you, Mr. Todd. If you'll excuse me now, I have a story to write. I trust I'll see you again."

"I trust you will," Todd agreed. He supposed Edmund would continue following him around, nosing into his business, as long as he was in Stick City.

Groseille said nothing. He didn't even give Todd another glance as he followed Edmund out.

Todd didn't like it. He didn't like them. Edmund was a sly little man full of innuendo, and Groseille was a glassy-eyed mystery. They could cause trouble. If Groseille had a knack for portraiture, he might be able to do a good likeness from memory. A likeness that could show up on WANTED posters if the law ever came into this affair.

A distinctive face, Groseille had said. Todd looked at his reflection in the back-bar mirror. It was becoming a sharply individual face. That was no advantage to a man in his position. He told himself that once he got his hands on a stake, he would do well to go into some other business.

Feeling an urgency, a need to be done with this affair and away from Stick City, he swallowed down the last piece of sandwich, gulped the remains of the beer, and left the saloon.

CHAPTER 7

Todd was thinking of failure. That was something he had never worried about in the old days. When he was young, working with the Colonel, he had felt himself invulnerable. Now he knew it was possible to fail.

He walked slowly past the bright lanterns of the saloons and on toward the houses hulking in the night. He paused a short distance from the Samson house. As he stood looking at it in the moonlight, he fingered the coins in his pocket. There weren't many left. He had spent lavishly, in keeping with his appearance. With what remained, he might be able to make it through a week here in the role he played. But he sure as hell wouldn't have enough to see him safely out of Stick City, safely to some distant hiding place, if the scheme should go wrong.

It was late for making calls, but Todd didn't think Millard Samson was abed yet. There were windows lit in the looming house, upstairs and down. And what the hell? He didn't like Millard Samson. He didn't care whether or not he woke the man.

He studied the house as he approached it. A fairly large and new building, quite stylish, with a porte-cochere on one side, a covered veranda running across the front and along the other side, and corner turrets rising above. There would undoubtedly be stained glass in some of the windows, and at least one marble fireplace. Samson seemed to be doing well in Stick City. But, then, it wasn't hard to be a large frog in such a very small pond.

Todd knew a lot about Millard Samson. Far more than

Samson was aware of. Todd had spent money for information, as insurance of a sort.

He knew Millard Samson was the brother of a prominent New York banker with whom Todd had been acquainted some years earlier. Millard was almost twenty years younger than the brother. He was a child of his parents' old age, and something of a nuisance to them. There were sisters, all much older than Millard, all well married now to men of substance, all in evidence in society.

The elder brother had won distinction as an officer in the Army of the Potomac during the Civil War. Millard had been too young for the war. He had graduated military school in the spring of sixty-five. He'd had no chance to match his brother's accomplishments in the field.

Commissioned, he had spent a little more than a year with the Army during the reconstruction in Georgia. Then he had been transferred to a frontier outpost. Instead of distinguishing himself in the wars with the Indians, he had soon resigned his commission under obscure circumstances.

For a while he had dabbled in various ventures without notable success. A partnership in a St. Louis hotel had proved profitable. Selling his share, he had tried his hand at the banking business, like his big brother.

His first bank failed. The second, somewhat smaller, succeeded. But Samson sold it, again under cloudy circumstances. Coming to Stick City he tried again. Here, he was prospering.

He had married in Georgia, taking a wife described as beneath him. She died on the frontier. He had remarried since coming to Stick City.

According to the housemaid who had told Todd this part of the story, the second wife was evidently a gift from the big brother. She was a woman of excellent breeding, from an old, established but financially troubled New York family. Samson had visited his brother in New York and returned to Stick City with the new wife. Shortly after that, loans from the older brother had solved the family's immediate financial problems.

It was easy to surmise the older Samson had bought the wife for Millard.

Then, on his most recent trip to New York, Millard Samson had bought himself James Todd Fox.

Todd walked up the gravel drive. The steps to the veranda were flanked by cast-iron greyhounds. He climbed the steps and looked at the fanlight over the door. It was stained glass. Very good glass, as best he could judge in the dim light. The brass handle of a mechanical doorbell invited him. He gave it a turn. Even through the thick oak of the door, he could hear its raucous clamor.

Long, still moments followed. He stood waiting. At last the glow of a lamp brightened the glass over the door. A bolt clicked. The door edged open a crack. The lamp was sitting behind the person who had opened the door. Todd could see no detail of the face that confronted him.

The voice was female, small, wispy, and uncertain. "Yes?"

He produced a card and thrust it through the crack. "Mr. James Todd to see Mr. Millard Samson."

"Just a minute, please, sir." The door closed. The bolt clicked into place.

Todd waited.

Soon the bolt clicked again. This time the door swung wide. The woman who had opened it—just a girl, really—wore a flowered nightcap and a chintz wrapper that she clutched closed at the throat. The face that looked up at Todd had the too-small, pinched-bone structure of long childhood hunger. The soft flesh padding the bone told him she was no longer hungry, but the wide, deep eyes still had the fearful look that went with the slight bone. She was no taller than his chin, narrow through the shoulders, with only a slight suggestion of breasts evident under the wrapper. There was an incomplete look about her. Her life, her being, her whole story showed in that face and thin frame. She was born to scrimp, to scrape, to serve. She would never escape that fate.

For a moment, images of Five Points, of New York's worst slums, crowded into Todd's mind. He could almost smell the stench of the streets. The taste of memory was as dry as fear in his mouth.

"Mr. Samson is in his study," the maid said. "He'll see you there. Please follow me, sir."

She picked up the lamp from the hall table and led him through a wide arch that separated the entryway from the front parlor. He glanced around at the parlor, at the dull gleam of polished mahogany, the quick glitter of brass ormolu and fine porcelains, the mellow sheen of the marble facings on the fireplace. Underfoot, the carpet was soft and deep. Even the scent of the room was expensive.

Across the parlor, a door stood open, spilling out lamplight. Through it, Todd could see a flat-topped desk. Millard Samson sat behind the desk, watching the maid lead Todd to the doorway.

At the door, she curtsied awkwardly and told Samson, "Mr. Todd, sir."

"Thank you," Samson grunted, the words merely a dismissal.

The girl left.

Samson rose as Todd entered the room. He was in his shirtsleeves, with his vest open. The shirt was linen, the vest Cheviot. Automatically he raised a hand to button the vest. He caught himself at it and stopped short. It was a small gesture, but it said clearly he did not feel his visitor was worthy of even such a simple propriety.

Samson was a tall man, almost as tall as Todd. His slenderness made him look taller. It was a whippet leanness, corded and sleek. The nose that dominated his face was long and thin, arched just a bit too much to be classic. Under it, his mouth was wide, thin-lipped, mobile. Long sideburns framed his shaven jaw. His hair, thick and wavy, was the color of pewter. It glistened as if he polished it daily. Eyes not much darker than the hair crowded the bridge of his nose, peering from his face as if through a mask.

His stance, his expression, his every gesture, had the casual elegance of aristocracy. The look of overbred, decadent aristocracy that appalled the proletariat and awed the *nouveaux riches*. Todd thought that Don Edmund with his pitiful pretensions must burn with envious hatred of Millard Samson.

Samson stood behind the broad-topped Chippendale kneehole desk as if it were a barrier between Todd and himself. Despite Todd's inch or so advantage in height, Samson managed to look down his regal nose. In a tone appropriate for addressing an unsatisfactory servant he said, "Well?"

There was a chair in front of the desk, a little to one side of it. A stiff, wooden chair not intended to put its occupant at ease. With a disregard for the proprieties as total and intentional as Samson's tone, Todd dropped uninvited into the chair. He slumped indolently in a way that said clearly he didn't give a damn about Samson's opinion of him.

A humidor sat on the corner of the desk. Samson watched coldly as Todd flipped up the lid and helped himself to a cigar. Todd didn't particularly want the cigar. He simply wanted to annoy Samson. He knew that was poor policy. He was presently dependent on Samson. But the man's damned superior attitude irked him. He could see no difference between the two of them, except that he had slipped once and been caught, and Samson hadn't. Otherwise, behind the masks they wore they were both thieves, and Samson knew it as well as Todd did.

Todd lit the cigar, sighed a puff of smoke across the desk, and met Samson's pewter eyes.

"Well?" Samson repeated, every subtle coloring of tone exactly as before.

A sudden sound in the parlor stopped Todd's reply. It was a woman's footfall, a bolder step than the maid's. Samson looked past Todd at the doorway.

"Millard, I heard the doorbell," the woman said.

"I have a visitor," Samson answered, his voice controlled and casually pleasant. With a hesitation so brief that Todd hardly caught the word as an afterthought, Samson added, "dear."

With a quick ease, Todd slipped from the arrogant posture he had assumed. Rising from the chair, he was in character again, a gentleman of manners. He bowed as the woman came to the doorway.

She must have come down from upstairs. Todd guessed she had been abed, perhaps reading by the lamp he had seen glowing through an upper window. Unlike the maid, she hadn't simply thrown a wrapper over her night clothes at the sound of the bell. She had slipped into a tea gown of French Henrietta in a shade of blue that reflected the piercing blue of her eyes. Her hair, braided for bed, had been twisted into a coil at the back of her head, and loose wisps were caught up with combs. Her face, a little too long and thin for the impromptu hairdo, was fashionably pallid. Her mouth was narrow, with full lips, her natural expression suggesting a pout. She looked Todd over as she came toward him, intending to be introduced. Her gaze was appraising, and approving.

Samson had no alternative. Graciously he said, "My dear, this is Mr. James Todd—" The inflection was wrong. He had almost added *Fox*. But he caught the word and swallowed it unspoken. He turned to Todd. "My wife, Galatea."

"The former Galatea Barr?" Todd sounded impressed. "Your servant, madame."

She smiled, flattered. "You know me, Mr. Todd?"

"I have met your father. I know your reputation"—he saw the flicker of her eyelids at that word—"as one of New York's fairest flowers. I understand a hundred hearts were broken when Galatea Barr left Astor Place."

He kissed the hand she extended, then looked into her face. Oils and creams had kept her complexion smooth, but the texture of the skin under her eyes and at the throat betrayed the fact that she had worn that face well over forty years.

Her eyes met his. In this moment, they were pleased eyes, and just a bit predatory. More often, he thought, they would be weary and harried. Galatea Barr Samson was not a happy woman.

"I believe Mr. Todd has some matters of business he came here to discuss," Samson said to his wife. His tone told her to go back upstairs.

"Certainly." She smiled at Todd. "I do hope you'll call socially, Mr. Todd. We have very few guests from the outside world here in Stick City."

"I'd be delighted," Todd answered. He could sense Samson's disapproval. Samson wasn't enjoying this game at all.

When Galatea's footsteps had faded up the stairs, Todd faced Samson again. And again, neither was in the role of gentleman.

Once more Samson demanded, "Well?"

"I saw Amos McRae today," Todd said.

"So?"

"I'm going to need more money."

"What?"

"It takes bait to catch a fish. The bigger the fish you're after, the bigger bait you need."

"I'm not after a damned whale," Samson said. "I'm after a backwoods yahoo who thinks he's a cattle baron."

"I've dangled the bait but I have to have time to set the hook," Todd answered. "I have to keep up appearances until he's been landed."

"I gave you money in New York. I gave you plenty."

"It takes a lot." Todd leaned forward to flick the cigar ash into the receiver on the desk.

Samson eyed the ring Todd wore. "Is that gold?"

Todd nodded.

"Gold!" Samson grunted, mingling anger and disgust. "I suppose you bought that with the expense money I gave you."

"With some of it. I also bought clothing and passage West and other necessities."

"Is a *gold* ring a necessity?"

"Yes."

"Why?"

"Would you have preferred brass? Something that would have turned my finger green and screamed *fake?*"

"Is a ring necessary?"

Todd glanced significantly at Samson's hand. A small, tasteful diamond set in gold adorned one finger. "It's usual."

"It's extravagant," Samson said.

"You can't skimp on details in something like this," Todd told him. "You can't afford to. Not if you want to succeed. Don't worry. You'll get your investment back, and a healthy profit as well."

"I'd better!"

"I know my business."

Sharply, Samson said, "You have failed before."

"Once," Todd admitted. "Only once."

"You could fail again."

"I won't."

"But you *could.*"

"This plan is *yours*, Samson," Todd said coldly. "The idea is *yours*. I only worked out the details. You left the details to me because it's my business. Either you'll trust me with them and go along with me all the way, or I quit."

"You can't quit."

"I don't intend to let you jeopardize the plan. My neck is out a lot further than yours."

"Dammit, Fox, I hired you to *make* money for me, not to *spend* it for me."

"You have to spend it to make it. You know that. And I would recommend you remember my name is *Todd*, not *Fox.*"

Samson was taken aback by his slip. He glanced around. Defensively he said, "No one can hear us here."

"The next time, someone might be listening."

"I don't want a *next time*. I don't want you to come here until you've completed this business."

"Give me my money and I'll go now."

Samson hesitated. With a sigh he said, "How much?"

"Two hundred should do nicely."

"*Two hundred!*"

"You want Amos McRae. You want to skin him and hang his head over your mantelpiece. You don't bring down a quarry like that with a peashooter."

"He's just a backwoods yahoo. It should be child's play."

"Then why don't you take him yourself?" Todd said blandly. "Why ring me in?"

"Damn you, Fox! You don't appreciate what I'm doing for you. You don't remember where I found you."

Todd remembered well enough. But bedamned if he'd let Samson cow him. Shrugging, he turned his back on the banker and started for the door.

"Where do you think you're going?" Samson demanded.

"Out. Away from here."

"Back to New York? Back to Five Points?"

Todd didn't flinch. Jaw taut, he kept walking.

"Two hundred's too damned much!" Samson called at him.

He stopped then and looked over his shoulder. "Do you want this thing done right?"

"Yes."

When he had set the figure at two hundred, Todd had expected to haggle. He had supposed he would settle for one hundred. But Samson had antagonized him. And now he could sense that Samson was conceding. Firmly he said, "Two hundred."

There was still anger in Samson's voice as he said, "Wait in the parlor. I'll get it for you."

So there was a safe hidden in the study, Todd thought as Samson closed the door between them. But safes weren't his line. He stood waiting.

Suddenly light glimmered in the hallway. The maid came tiptoeing into view. At the sight of Todd, she gave a small squeal. Then, very apologetically, she said, "I'm sorry, sir. I heard a door close. I thought you'd gone."

"I'll be gone in a few minutes," he told her.

She looked past him at the closed study door, puzzled as to

why her master would have shut the door on a guest who was so obviously a gentleman.

Impulsively, Todd said, "I think he doesn't like me very much.

She almost smiled. But it wouldn't have been proper. Todd supposed Samson insisted his household help be proper at all times.

"Excuse me, sir," the girl said, making her awkward little curtsy. She started to back away.

Todd felt like stopping her and talking with her a moment. But that was impossible. He gave her a nod, and she hurried away.

The study door finally opened. Samson stood with the money in his hand. He held it out at arm's length as if he were afraid something about Todd might be contagious. That was laughable. When Samson found him, Todd had been working at an honest job. The only honest job he'd ever held in his life. Samson had taken him away from it. Made a criminal of him again. And now *he* was the leper and Samson the clean one.

The butt of the cigar was still in his hand. He flicked ashes on the carpet. He thought of dropping the butt there, grinding it in with his heel. But the maid was the one who would have to clean it up and try to restore the damaged spot. She was the one who would suffer, not Samson.

Todd felt sorry for her. Sorry for all the ones like her, who were doomed to follow the ones like Samson, cleaning up after them, emptying their chamber pots, shoveling manure in their stables, and knowing the only end of it all was the grave.

He realized he was feeling sorry for himself, for the fact that there was no one following *him*. No one jumped at his beck and call to empty his chamber pot.

The world looked a lot different from the bottom than from the top, he thought.

Pocketing the money, he gave Samson a sardonic grin and turned his back.

"Don't come back here," Samson reminded him as he stepped to the door.

Walking into the night, back to the hotel, he pondered the different views from the top of the world and the bottom of it. He wondered about the view from the middle. That was Asia McRae's view, he thought. And he wondered how her bright, hazel eyes looked on life.

CHAPTER 8

It was another hot, sticky morning that offered no promise of improvement. Not a trace of a cloud marred the burning blue of the sky.

Todd cursed his cravat as he tied it. He felt strangled by it. Smothered under the clothing he wore. And the role he played.

He wondered if he had lost his touch. It seemed he no longer had the temperament for this kind of work. It was no good, no fun any more. He told himself, once he had his stake he would have to find some other way of living. But what the hell did he know except working swindles and swinging a manure shovel?

He didn't feel like breakfast. He went directly to the livery stable, collected the mount McRae had loaned him, and rode off. At the ridge beyond town, he met a small breeze. It helped some. Away from town, the heat didn't seem so oppressive.

By the time he reached the bridge, he was certain he was being followed again. Edmund, he supposed. It didn't matter.

He was better than halfway to the ranch when he saw a rider coming toward him. Even at the distance, he recognized Asia McRae.

It was pleasant watching her ride toward him. She sat her sidesaddle with an ease that was as graceful as it was informal. Nothing at all like the proper seat for a lady of society riding to the hounds. But nice. Very nice.

As she came up to him, she halted and greeted him with a smile. Her face was flushed from her gallop. Her shining eyes were like polished gemstones in the plain setting of her face.

He thought suddenly that it was a very tasteful setting for them, offering no distraction from their special beauty.

Smiling, he returned her greeting.

"We were afraid you might not be able to find the way." She sounded a little apologetic, a little embarrassed. "So I decided to ride out and meet you."

"I appreciate your thoughtfulness, Miss McRae," he said, wondering if it had been her own idea, or her mother's. He found himself hoping the idea had been hers. And he noticed she had made a concession to his visit today. Instead of a loose calico blouse, she had on a lacy ecru shirtwaist. A pretty, feminine one that fitted more closely than the blouse had. He realized her breasts were rather full. Very nicely shaped. Appealing. She had a good body, he thought. And lovely eyes. And under that coat of tan, her face wasn't really so plain as he had first thought.

"Please call me Asia," she said.

He answered, "That would hardly be proper."

"Must one always be proper? Don't you get tired of always being proper, Mr. Todd?"

He cocked a brow at her, wondering just how improper she was willing to be. But there was a directness about her that suggested she meant no innuendoes.

"Some of the proprieties seem so foolish," she said. "I mean trivial, useless things like that suit coat you're wearing."

"What's wrong with my coat?"

"It's far too heavy for this weather. You're simply broiling in it. Don't deny it. Your face is dripping. But you keep that foolish coat on just because you consider it proper."

"Because others consider it proper," he admitted.

She smiled again. "Around here, none of our menfolk wear coats in the summer except on special occasions and Sundays. We've all seen our gentlemen in their shirtsleeves. There isn't a woman for miles around who'd be offended if you took it off. Why don't you take it off and be more comfortable?"

For an instant, he felt completely flustered. The coat was a part of his disguise, a part of the masquerade. But she was right about it being hellishly hot. He hesitated, tempted to shed it.

She nudged her horse up close and reached for his mount's bridle. "Here. I'll hold your horse while you do it. He's not usually skittish, but you never know."

He peeled the coat. And found that he felt oddly naked without it, as if it had been his only defense. As if she might actually see him for himself instead of the gentleman he played.

They rode on, side by side, talking about the weather, the countryside, the cattle business, and Asia herself.

He discovered she was educated, well-read and well informed about the world beyond Stick City. Despite the briefness of her stay at the ladies' academy, she knew the manners of society. She just chose to ignore some of them.

She was, Todd decided, a unique individual. And an interesting one.

By the time they reached the ranch, he had forgotten about his coat altogether. He was completely comfortable in his shirtsleeves.

Amos McRae was waiting on the veranda. His horse was saddled and ready at the hitch rail. Politely, he invited Todd inside for a drink and a rest before they rode on.

Todd could see his eagerness to be on the way. He accepted the drink, but he made it a quick one. Then they mounted up and headed for the spring.

From the Pitchfork gate, they rode cross-country into the badlands. Amos led. Where the trail was wide enough, Asia rode at Todd's side. But, for the most part, they were in defiles barely wide enough for a rider to keep his knees safe, or else scrambling up and down rocky outthrusts that demanded the full attention of the rider as well as the horse.

They reached Stick Creek at a point well above the dam. A place where it was a small rush of water tumbling down a rocky bed in shattering cascades. They paused to let the horses drink.

Asia pulled off her Stetson and wiped her forehead with a

kerchief. She told Todd, "People call this Stick Creek, but properly it's The River Styx."

It was a fitting name, he thought. It was hot as hell here among the rocks. Burning hot. Hot enough to bake a man's brains out. His collar and cravat seemed to be choking him. He was grateful that Asia had talked him out of the coat. He wished she'd suggest abandoning the collar, too.

Amos wiped his own brow. Sounding put out, he said, "Even the government surveyors never got the right of it. They set it down on their maps as Stick Creek and now it'll never get straight."

Todd didn't care. It was too hot for him to care. He merely nodded.

Asia explained, "Pa named the river."

Amos was happy to talk about it. "When I first came out here I was all full of piss and vinegar and free-school education. I figured it was my right to name it all. These badlands looked like a heap of leftovers from the building of hell, and it sure felt like hell, so I named this water run The River Styx. But a lot of the folk who came after me never even heard of the old Greeks, and didn't know any of the old Greek stories. No matter what I said, they changed the name into words they knew. *Stick Creek.* Damned ridiculous name for a river."

"Even a little one like this," Asia said.

Todd nodded again, wondering how much farther to the spring. He longed to be back at the ranch, in the shade, with a tall drink in his hand. Or back at the hotel where he could strip to the skin. As he bobbed his head, the stiff collar scraped at his neck, chafing it, and the sweat stung bitterly.

Asia went on, "Last year that idiot Don Edmund ran an article in his paper about how it was really an Indian name. According to his story, the Indians put up a pole as a landmark to show where there was water, and they called this The River with the Stick in It."

"God knows what old gaffer gave him that tale," Amos said. "Some of these old-timers around here will spin you windies until a week come Christmas and never let one word

of truth slip in. They'll tell you there's Indian gold hid in
these badlands, and old Spanish treasure, and even loot that
Quantrill's raiders stowed here during the war." He suddenly
cocked an eye at Todd. "Son, nobody's been leading you up
the path with lost-treasure tales, have they?"

Todd shook his head and worked up a chuckle. The collar
cut painfully at his neck. The chuckle was weak. Forced. He
could feel Amos's eyes on him, full of suspicion, as if questioning his whole story about a spa and a railroad. He answered, "For every man who finds a lost treasure, hundreds go
broke or die trying. I prefer better odds than that."

"I hope so," Amos grunted, lifting rein.

They scrambled the horses up a clutter of rock, onto a flat
that would be the bottom of the water run when the creek
was full. As they rode, Todd thought through details of the
plan. He would have to start throwing them at Amos to keep
the rancher convinced the plan was legitimate. He was thank-
ful he had worked them all out beforehand. It would be
difficult to think straight in this damned heat.

Asia was riding at his side, "When I was a little girl, Cole
and I used to come out here hunting the treasures. All we ever
found were some Indian relics and, once, an old shilling. But
it was fun to hunt."

"I became involved in a treasure hunt of a sort once in
France," Todd heard himself say.

"Oh? What happened?" Asia seemed really interested.

Wondering why the hell he had brought it up, Todd said,
"It proved to be a swindle. The perpetrators ended up in
prison."

"I hope you didn't lose anything," she said.

"More than I'd care to admit." There was a sharper edge in
his voice than he had intended. A suggestion of old pain. He
smiled at Asia, trying to make it seem unimportant.

She returned the smile with sympathy.

He felt curiously tempted to tell her the whole thing. A
damned insane impulse. He told himself the heat really was
cooking his brains.

"Is it much farther?" he asked.

"About ten minutes."

The River Styx led them across a wide-open flat of sand and rock, then into another defile. The floor was a shallow slope. As they rode up it, the walls grew higher and closer. The bottom became so narrow that the creek covered it. The horses waded in the water. The riders' knees brushed rock in the tight, twisting turns. But at least it was shaded here, and there was relief from the intensity of the heat.

Around a bend, the defile widened. And then it opened out into a box canyon.

It was a small canyon that looked like it might have been a lake bed once, with a river rushing out of it cutting the defile. Now it was dry, but not arid like the surrounding badlands. Water welled from a crack about head-high in one wall. It streamed down over worn rock streaked with the bright colors of mineral deposits, splashed into a cup in the rock, and spilled out into a placid pool. A gully carried the overflow from the pool in a meander across the canyon to the defile.

In the spring floods, the whole canyon bottom would be covered with water. Now it was covered with grass, long and lush and green. The sweet scent of the grass was stronger than the faint sulphur odor of the spring. In the shadows of the canyon walls, the air was cool and fresh. Overhead, the sky was a perfect blue.

Todd breathed deeply as he surveyed the scene before him. The canyon wasn't large enough to be called majestic, but it was beautiful. After the hell of the badlands, it was overwhelmingly beautiful. A piece of paradise.

He rode up to the edge of the pool and dismounted. Squatting, he touched the water. The touch was delight. The spring was slightly warm, about the temperature of the air. He held his hand in it, wishing he could plunge his whole body into it. Soothe the aches of the ride and the chafing sweat stings. Rest in the water's caress.

"How do you like it?" Asia asked him.

He rose and turned toward her. Sincerely he said, "It's perfect."

"The Indians said there were good spirits living here," Amos told him. "They said that water had real good medicine."

Remembering there was a job to be done, Todd sighed. He collected himself, and in the voice of the man he was supposed to be he asked, "What do you think?"

Amos hesitated. A little embarrassed, he admitted, "I've drunk some of it when my bones ached."

"Did it help?"

"Can't say it did. Can't say it didn't either. The aches would go away for a while, then come back again. They do that anyway. I took a lot of that water when this busted pin of mine was healing. It still healed crooked." Amos tapped his lame leg. Then, thoughtfully, he added, "The water tastes powerful enough, it ought to have some good in it."

Todd scooped water in his hand. He sniffed it, then sampled it. Asia grinned at his grimace.

"Powerful," he agreed. It tasted of iron and sulphur and lime and God knew what else. He scanned the walls of the canyon. "You hold legal title to all of this, Mr. McRae?"

Amos nodded. "Free and clear. A long time back, I actually did find a trace of color in the badlands. I figured I'd found my fortune. Raised the cash and bought the whole shebang outright. Panned a while and took about six ounces of gold. Then I brought in a mining engineer to look it over. He told me I'd pretty much cleaned it out. There's some silver, but it's such low grade it ain't worth the taking and hauling."

With a teasing glance at her father, Asia said, "Some folks call these badlands 'McRae's Folly.' "

Amos gave a grunt. "I never heard them called that."

"Of course they don't say it to your face," she answered.

"It's got water," he protested. "It's got one damned spring that's never gone dry."

"The cows don't like the taste of it," she said.

"They'll drink it, they get thirsty enough." He turned to Todd again, and changed the subject. "Well, what do you think of it? Would it make a good spa?"

"The water seems excellent," Todd admitted. He pointed toward the rim of the canyon. "Is there a way to get up there from here?"

"Game trails. You want to go up there?"

Todd didn't really want to go. He thought he would like to spend the rest of the day right there in the canyon by the pool, enjoying that little piece of paradise. But there was a job to do.

He nodded.

Amos led the way. The game trail was well-worn, not difficult for nimble horses. At the top they reached a plateau higher than most of the surrounding land. From the canyon's brink, a man could look down at the spring, or out across the badlands to the woods and rolling hills of the cattle range. Far beyond the hills a row of distant ridges stood, a misty purple against the sky. And on the height there was a breeze that cut the heat.

Todd sat his horse, gazing around him at the vista. He heard himself whisper in awe, "Magnificent!"

Amos grunted.

"Will it serve your purpose, Mr. Todd?" Asia asked.

Quite honestly, he told her, "It has the making of a fine spa. You could put the main buildings here, and a bathhouse by the spring. Build a fountain and a tile pool—no—no, I don't think I'd do that. I'd leave it the way it is. Rustic and natural. I'd make the buildings rustic and natural, too. Fit them into the scenery. I'd bring the railroad in from that direction"—he pointed off to his left—"where it wouldn't intrude on the view. Grade a carriage road up here and bring the guests from the cars in an omnibus. I'd want to give it all the comforts of civilization without any unnecessary trappings. Keep the guests aware of the wild, rugged nature of the land—"

He stopped abruptly, suddenly aware that he had become caught up in his own game. He realized that he actually would like to carry the plan through to completion, really build a spa there. It saddened him to think that he was only working a swindle. And that feeling was unsettling.

He glanced at Asia. Her smile, confident and trusting and as lovely in its way as the canyon, was even more unsettling.

He wished to hell he were somewhere else. Anywhere else. Even in that damned French prison again.

CHAPTER 9

Sarah McRae came out onto the veranda as the riders halted in front of the house. She greeted Todd with her eager smile, and insisted he stay for dinner.

He was weary from the ride, and vaguely depressed. He would rather have gone back to town, to the solitude of his own thoughts. But there was business to be done, a future to be considered. He had to play this role through to completion.

Once Sarah had his promise that he would stay, she tugged her husband off on some obscure matter. Todd thought he saw her give Amos a sly wink. The two of them disappeared into the house, leaving Todd and Asia alone on the veranda.

"Mother's a matchmaker at heart," Asia said. Her tone was teasing, her smile self-conscious and a little wistful. "I'm afraid she thinks you're a very eligible gentleman."

Todd found it difficult to respond, to match the lightness of her tone. His words were a lie. He almost wished they weren't. "Perhaps I am. Are you a very eligible young lady?"

"Mother thinks so. She's been trying to push me off on one young man or another since I was sixteen."

He lifted his brows. "And she hasn't succeeded yet!"

"She hasn't tried it with the right young man yet." As she spoke, Asia turned to gaze off into the distance. She had taken off her hat. The sunlight glimmered on her hair, putting bright sparks of gold in it. Todd felt an urge to touch it. He wondered if she wanted him to. But it wasn't something James R. Todd of Richmond, Virginia, would do on such short acquaintance.

She seemed to be waiting. He felt the awkwardness of his silence. Before, words had always come easily for him. At this moment, he searched fruitlessly for the right ones.

She spoke up. "Do you think you'll be able to work something out with Pa about the Indian spring, Mr. Todd?"

It was a relief to change the subject. "I don't see why not. It's a good spring. If he doesn't insist on unreasonable terms, we should be able to reach an agreement."

"And you're certain the railroad will build into Stick City?"

"If they have reason enough, they will."

She turned her face to him again. Her enthusiasm shone in her eyes. "Do you have any idea what the railroad would mean to us here in Stick City, Mr. Todd? Do you know anything about the cattle business?"

"Not much."

"It isn't easy. The market is always up and down. If you've had a good year and you've got a good herd to put on the market, so does everybody else. The prices drop. Unless you're first at the railroad with your beef, you don't get a decent price. Then, if you have a bad year, a long dry spell, everyone loses stock. There's not so much beef to glut the market and the prices are good. But you don't have much beef to sell. The longer and harder the drive to the railroad is, the more meat you walk off the cattle and the more stock you lose on the trail. Sometimes you lose men. Sometimes it costs more to get your beef to the railroad than you're paid for them when you get them there." She paused. "I lost a brother on the trail."

He felt the sadness in her and asked her, "Why do you stay in the cattle business? Surely you could sell the ranch for a fair price and go somewhere else. Do something else."

She gave him a small, wistful smile. "It's hard to say, Mr. Todd. Why does anyone stay in a hard business? It's *our* business. This is our home. Our place in the world. We'll stick with it if we can."

He nodded slightly, wondering why he was what he was, and what it would be like to have a place in the world.

"But with the railroad right here," she went on, "we wouldn't have to drive the trail. In a bad year, a dry year like this, when the prices are high, we'd be able to put our beef on the market without walking them down to skin and bone. We could get the top prices available. It would mean a great deal to us. Not just Pa, but all the ranchers here. And not just the ranchers, either. It would mean a lot to the whole town. It would make it easier to bring in our supplies. It would bring stock to the stores, and customers to them. The people coming to your spa would mean business for everyone here. It could make a real city out of Stick City."

"Yes." Todd had to remind himself that what happened to Stick City, to the ranchers, to Amos McRae and his family, was none of his concern. He had a swindle to carry out here, and for him that was the whole of it.

Asia was a good subject. She was doing an excellent job of selling herself on the deal. If Amos did as well, there would be no problems. Todd knew he should mention the capital investment to Asia. He should press her gently toward the idea that the spa would be even more profitable to the area if it were locally financed. He should start her thinking that her father could put up a part of the investment needed to build the spa.

But he couldn't bring himself to it. Not now.

Asia was saying, "Of course, Pa will have to talk to the other ranchers."

He looked askance at her. "What do you mean?"

"Pa wouldn't agree to bringing in the spa unless the others agreed. There's a lot of tension here now. If Pa made a move like that against the will of the others, it could set off trouble."

"But there's bound to be some opposition," Todd told her. "There's always someone ready to object to anything."

"Like that Don Edmund." She spoke the name as if it had

a sour taste to it. "He's certain to fight us. He owns the Stick City *Sentinel*. That's our local newspaper. Have you seen it yet?"

"I read an editorial in the current issue."

"The one attacking us?"

He nodded.

She gave an angry toss of her head. "Don Edmund is a fool. He's a troublemaker, always looking to stir up people against one thing or another. That's his stock in trade. Trouble. He reports it and he makes it."

"He accused your father of trying to drive the small ranchers out of business." Todd found himself wondering about that. He could understand men who wanted to wipe out their competition and absorb other business operations into their own. He had dealt with that kind, turning their greed against them, clipping them with their own shears. He had never thought there were any other kind. But Amos McRae seemed different. The difference puzzled him. He said, "Your father did dam the Stick River, didn't he?"

"He didn't stop it completely. If he had wanted to dry up the other ranches that use that water, he would have built the dam high enough to hold it all back. He's keeping the river flowing. He's doling out the water so that it will last for Pitchfork and for everybody else!"

She seemed sincere about it. And perhaps it was true. Todd sold men lies. He thought it should be just as simple to sell them the truth. "Can't he explain that to the others?"

"He tries. When he talks to them, they believe him. Then Edmund writes one of those highfalutin editorials of his and they believe him. They forget what Pa's done for this place. He's the one who got it started to begin with. He's the one who's kept it going through hard times. Pitchfork is the best customer the business people in town have. Pitchfork provides help when somebody needs it. Our riders run the trail drives. They give the other ranchers a hand. And right now it's Pitchfork money that's keeping some of those ranchers going!"

"Pitchfork money?"

"Pa had made loans to several ranchers. He's holding almost ten thousand dollars in mortgages right now, for a lot less interest than Mr. Samson's bank would ask."

"Lending money isn't always the best way to keep friends," Todd said. "Some people resent indebtedness."

She smiled slightly, understanding. "I know. Pa is one of them. But sometimes lending and borrowing are necessary. Especially in a business like ours. Some years back, Pa took a mortgage on Pitchfork to bring in some Durham breeding stock. It wasn't a big mortgage, not a fraction of what the ranch was worth. And Pa was paying it back regularly. Then the panic of seventy-three hit and we had some hard times. Pa couldn't keep up the payments. He had to go to Mr. Samson for an extension. Mr. Samson wouldn't give it to him. That— that—he tried to foreclose on Pa!"

That was interesting. Todd knew Millard Samson hated Amos McRae. He was beginning to see reasons. He asked, "What happened?"

"Pa managed to borrow money in Dadeston. He paid off Mr. Samson, and hasn't had a civil word for him since. Now we do all our banking in Dadeston. And Mr. Samson hasn't had a civil word for Pa since Pa started lending money here. I think, if it weren't for Pa, Mr. Samson would have foreclosed half the small ranches around here by now."

The pattern was taking shape for Todd. It was Millard Samson who wanted to run the competition out of business. Samson who wanted to take over. Amos McRae stood in his way. So Samson was determined to destroy McRae, and Todd was his chosen instrument. Thinking of Edmund's editorials, Todd wondered if the newspaperman belonged to Samson.

He asked, "Do you suppose Samson holds a mortgage on the Stick City *Sentinel?*"

She cocked a brow at him. "You think Mr. Samson is behind Edmund's attacks on us?"

"It occurred to me."

"I don't know. Edmund wouldn't need anybody to push him into attacking us. Or anyone else. He's a born trouble-maker. And a *cad*." She sounded as if she spoke from personal knowledge.

"He's insulted you?"

"He's *insulted* half the women in the county. The married ones as well as the unmarried ones."

"I could call him out for you," Todd heard himself tell her.

She eyed him curiously, uncertain whether or not he was in earnest.

He wondered the same thing. He had spoken impulsively. He disliked Don Edmunds, and he'd stood on the field of honor in the past for no better reason. But it wasn't any pleasure. Nothing he would do now if he could avoid it. And dueling was illegal in this country. A man could get himself into a lot of trouble. It wouldn't be wise to take the chance. A duel could hurt the swindle. Maybe ruin it completely. It could get Todd killed.

But he knew that if she said *yes*, he would do it for her.

She shook her head. Trying to give her words a lightness of tone, she said, "A gentleman only calls out another *gentleman*, doesn't he?"

"Yes."

"Don Edmund would hardly qualify as a *gentleman*." As she spoke she turned away from Todd, looking into the distance.

The sun caught sparks in her hair again. He gazed at her hair, at her back, at the line of her shoulder. He looked down at the curve of her waist into hip, and the drape of her skirt. He could understand a man acting the cad with her. His hands flexed with wanting to touch her, to hold her.

The silence growing between them was awkward and unsettling. With a jerk of his head, he pulled his eyes away from her. He glanced around, hunting a new subject for conversation. Something innocuous.

A bird wheeled in the sky above the badlands. Its wings

were spread motionless as it rode an unseen air current. It soared with a wild freedom, a pure grace and beauty that he admired and envied.

He asked, "Is that an eagle?"

She started as if she had been far away in her thoughts. Scanning the sky, she spotted the bird. "It's a buzzard."

"A vulture?"

"Yes."

It would be, he thought darkly. From a distance, it appeared a thing of beauty. Up close, one would see that it was actually a thing of ugliness and filth. A living lie.

As he watched, the vulture dived and disappeared behind the ridges. He wondered if it had found something dead to prey on. And then he asked himself if it was *preying* to destroy a dead thing, to clean the earth of carrion. Or was it only *preying* when you destroyed something alive, something vital with hopes and dreams.

He brought himself up short with a silent curse. His thoughts were running in strange ways. He had never been bothered by conscience before. But he had never worked a swindle on people like the McRaes before. When he was working with the Colonel, his victims had always been rich, always people who could afford to lose. Always people whose concern was amassing more wealth no matter what the cost to anyone else. The Colonel's schemes had always held a hint of larceny, appealing to the basic dishonesty of his victims.

Todd had a feeling Amos McRae wasn't like that at all. Certainly Asia wasn't. No, Millard Samson was the one who should have been the victim of the swindle.

And Todd was bothered in a way that he had never been bothered before.

Asia turned toward him. Her eyes looked for his. He didn't meet them. She studied him a moment, as if she were searching for something particular in him. Then she glanced away.

When she spoke it was with a forced lightness, as if she too had dark thoughts she wanted to escape. "What does the R stand for?"

"R?" He frowned, not understanding.

"It is James R. Todd, isn't it?"

"Oh. Yes. R for Reynard."

"Reynard," she repeated after him. "That's French, isn't it?"

"More or less. It means 'Fox.'" He wondered why he had said that.

"Doesn't Todd mean something to do with foxes, too?"

"A tod is the brush, the fox's tail. They call a fox with a full brush a tod."

"*Reynard Todd.*" She smiled at him. "Is that just coincidence?"

"Maybe it's a joke," he said.

She looked at him in question.

It really had been a joke of sorts. In the foundling home he had been known simply as Jim. Then the Colonel took him apprentice. The Colonel told the officials of the home that he wanted to rear the boy as a manservant. He told the boy that he wanted a young cub to train as a fox. The name he had given the boy was James Todd Fox.

But it was under that name that Todd had been arrested. The name was no longer quite comfortable, so he had changed it slightly. Now he was James Reynard Todd. But he could hardly tell Asia that story.

Lamely he said, "I come from a long line of foxes, on both sides of the family."

He knew his tone was wrong, and he could see that the answer bothered her. He was afraid she was reading something in his face. He couldn't afford to be read. Turning away from her, he looked at the ranch buildings down range. He said, "Do you have many men working for Pitchfork?"

"It depends on the season. At roundup we hire more. Right now, we only have a few." Her voice was flat. Her thoughts weren't on the words.

Todd wanted to say something else. Something meaningless that would distract her from those thoughts. The Colonel had trained him in small talk. There had been a time when he was adept at witty, charming, Continental conversation. But that was a long time since. Before the years in prison. Before he had met Asia McRae. He could find nothing at all to say now.

Asia asked, "Mr. Todd, what's wrong?"

Everything, he thought. He said, "Is something wrong?"

"You seem very worried."

He nodded without knowing he did it. He was losing control of himself. Losing the feel of the character he played. He was letting the mask he wore slip.

Suddenly he felt as if there might be nothing at all behind that mask. There was no such person as James Reynard Todd. It was only a role, just as James Todd Fox had been a role. If he was to let the mask fall away completely, if he played no role at all, would he be anyone at all?

He was nothing, a shadow disguised as a man. He had no being but the roles he played. He was a creation, a figment of his own imagination. No, not even his own. He was a creation of the Colonel, a fraud and swindler who had shaped a boy into a reflection of himself.

He thought of the mechanical figures on the great clock of Nuremberg, run by weights and gears, striking the hour without knowing the hour. Painted puppets.

This was no good. He was thinking like a madman. He told himself he was just overtired. The long ride in the hot sun had exhausted him. Once he was rested, everything would be all right. He would be in control of himself again then.

But, for now, he couldn't go on facing Asia like this.

"I just remembered something," he said, and he could hear that he was almost stammering. That had never happened to him before. "I've got something I *have* to attend in town. I'll have to go. Now."

"But Ma is expecting you for dinner."

"I'm terribly sorry. I'll have to apologize to her. But I *can't* stay now."

He said his good-bys to Sarah and Amos while Asia had a
fresh horse saddled for him. He took his leave of Asia after he
had mounted up. He did it stiffly, much too formally.

She stood watching him, a small, puzzled frown creasing
her forehead, as he rode away.

CHAPTER 10

As he rode away from the ranch house, Todd had the feeling that he was being watched. He knew Asia still stood on the veranda watching him, but this was something different. This was a sense of spying eyes boring his back. Accusing eyes. A damned unpleasant feeling. He wondered if it might be the feeling of conscience.

Throwing the horse into a gallop, he tried to outrun the feeling. When he reached the Pitchfork gate, he slowed his pace. The sense of spying eyes was gone. But he felt no relief. He simply felt hollow. Empty. Unhappy.

The road ahead led to Stick City, and he didn't want to go there. He wasn't sure where he wanted to go, or what he wanted to do. Just rest, he thought. But not in that ugly, stifling hole of a hotel room.

He turned off the road, drifting, thinking he would turn back and go on to the hotel in a little while. After all, there wasn't anywhere else to go.

Then he realized he was guiding the horse toward the trail he had ridden that morning. The trail up to the Indian spring. And he knew that he would keep riding on. He would cross the burning hell of the badlands and find that little piece of paradise again. He would rest a while there in the beauty and solitude of the canyon.

At first the trail was easy. But as it twisted into the badlands, he had to hunt his way. Concentrating, he recalled landmarks. Watching the ground, he spotted signs of the earlier ride up.

There were deep shadows in the canyon when he reached

it. Cool, quiet shadows. Dismounting, he stretched and yawned and breathed the sweet scent of the lush grass.

His shoulders ached, his legs were stiff, and his whole body stung with sweat. He loosened his cravat, then pulled it off. Impulsively, he jerked off the collar, too. With the top buttons of his shirt open, he could feel the cool air on his chest. It was a good feeling. A free feeling. The idea of returning to town saddened him. He thought he would like to stay here alone forever.

He tied the horse to a small bush, then walked to the edge of the pool. Water gurgled out of the spring, splashed down the rocks, shattered the surface of the pond into rolling ripples. Hunkering, he dipped his fingers into the water. The ripples they made crossed the others, cutting patterns in the water. Clear, clean, inviting water. It really would make a good spa. A fine mineral bath. Well worth coming this far for.

He peeled his clothes and piled them neatly on the bank, then slid into the water.

It was a gentle caress against his skin, soft and relaxing. He stretched out, shoving away from the bank and swam to the other side of the pond, then turned and swam back again. He could feel the stiffness easing out of his muscles and the sense of weariness seeping away. Rolling over, he floated, and the water held him lazily, like a cloud in a dream. His thoughts drifted to other times, to pleasant times.

But one memory led to another, and he found himself thinking of Paris, of the Colonel, and of that last, damned swindle. The one that had gone sour and sent them both to prison. The Colonel had died there in prison. So had the illusion of a man named James Fox.

When he had served out his time, he was deported from France. As an American citizen, he was shipped to New York City. He was dumped there like so much jetsam, nameless and penniless. There had been nowhere to go from there, and no way to go.

Officially, the story had been suppressed. Too many impor-

tant people were involved. The newspapers had made scant
mention of it. But there was no suppressing gossip.

The arrest of two socially prominent gentlemen, and their
exposure as frauds and thieves, had been juicy scandal in the
wealthy international circles he and the Colonel had traveled.
The well-to-do of New York and Newport, of Saratoga
Springs and White Sulphur Springs, all traveled the same circles, all shared the same gossip. They knew his face. Now they
knew his trade. So there was no returning to old haunts, no
picking up where he had left off. And there were no old
friends to turn to. The friendships James Fox had made were
as false as his name.

The United States might have been his native land, but the
place he found himself in was strange to him. He might be
fluent in four languages, but he couldn't speak the gutter jar-
gon of Five Points and the Bowery. He might have manipu-
lated millionaires, but he couldn't shoplift or pick pockets.
He had no connections among ward heelers and hoodlums.
The best he could do was find work, and the best work he
could find was handling horses in an East Side brewery stable. There, he had been Jim Todd, and he hadn't given any
thought to whom Jim Todd might be. He had been too busy
simply surviving.

But someone had seen Jim Todd and recognized James
Fox. Some servant from a household where he had once been
a guest. The word spread below stairs, moved upstairs, and
circulated in society circles. The charming young fraud who
had made fools of too many people had gone down to his
comeuppance.

Millard Samson, in the city on business, had heard an old
but still tasty bit of gossip. He had seen it as more than just
an amusing story. Samson had hunted out Jim Todd to offer
him a stake and a game in the Far West, in a town where
people didn't make the Grand Tour or enjoy the watering
places of the wealthy. A town where few were likely ever to
have heard of James T. Fox, and none likely ever to have seen
his face.

He had been hungry. He had jumped at the chance. And Jim Todd of Five Points, New York, had become James Reynard Todd of Richmond, Virginia.

Now, here, he suddenly realized he didn't want to be James R. Todd. He didn't want to play out his life in lies, living with no more substance than a character in a drama, who ceased to exist when the curtain fell.

He wanted an existence of his own, an identity of his own.

But not shoveling manure from dawn to dark, sleeping in some damned filthy flea pit of a rented room up a back alley. Not drinking himself to sleep and waking to another day just like the day before. No, to escape that he had to have a stake. To earn a stake, he had to pull off this one more swindle. With money in his pocket he could go somewhere new, find a new name and a new way to live. With luck, he could find out if there was a man behind the illusion he lived.

Only—dammit—he didn't want to hurt the McRaes. Especially not Asia. He hated the thought of dulling the sparkle in those hazel eyes. He hated the thought of having those eyes see past the mask, of having them see him for an illusion and a thief.

But there was no other way. Either the McRaes lost, or he lost.

Twisting in the water, he caught a breath and dived. He cut down sharply, quickly, as if he hoped to escape his own thoughts. But the pool was shallow. Just a moment of diving and he reached the gravel bottom. His hands touched it. His fingers scraped as if he grabbed for something. They found only sand. And then the water was pushing him up, sending him back.

As he broke the surface, he heard his horse snort. He had left the horse contentedly nibbling the long grass. Now it stood with its head up, its ears pointed and its nostrils flared. It gazed at the entrance to the canyon expectantly.

Something was coming.

Todd knew it could be an animal coming to drink. Perhaps a bear or a cougar. Or it might be a man.

He scrambled for the bank. He had left the pocket pistol wrapped in his shirt. As he grabbed the shirt, the gun fell out. Dropping the shirt, he snatched up the pistol and leveled the muzzle at the mouth of the canyon.

The figure that appeared was a man on a horse.

Cole McRae.

Cole came slowly into the canyon. He halted, and shifted indolently in the saddle. His eyes on Todd were scornful of what he saw.

The Remington in Todd's hand was a little gun. Fully loaded, it weighed less than a pound. With a scant inch of barrel, it lacked accuracy. It had little punch at any distance. It was a gun for ladies and counterjumpers, a small gun for small emergencies.

Standing naked with the tiny pistol like a toy in his hand, Todd thought he must look a fool. He sure as hell felt like one.

Cole's eyes scanned him. They didn't settle on his face, but his chest. There was curiosity in them. Todd remembered the bullet scar. And the whip marks. He couldn't let Cole see his back. Bending at the knees, he reached for his shirt with his left hand.

"Let it lie," Cole said.

Todd ignored the order. He scooped up the shirt. As he straightened, he saw Cole's hand slap at his hip. It came up thumbing back the hammer of a very large revolver. Todd could hear the sharp click of the sear as it caught.

Suddenly the muscles of Todd's jaw were tight. His mouth was dry and his palms were damp. He could feel the pounding of his heart, fast and angry against his chest. His hand wanted to trigger the Remington, to answer Cole's threat in kind.

He held himself taut, understanding that for some reason Cole had tracked him here to challenge him. Instinctively, he wanted to fling back the challenge. To fight. But that was no good. He had to avoid trouble if he possibly could. Carrying off a swindle like this was a business of precarious balance.

One small misstep and he might have the whole thing collapsing on him, burying him in another damned prison cell.

He couldn't accept Cole's challenge. He couldn't escape it either. He had to play out this hand somehow.

He could read a smoldering anger in Cole's face, but he didn't think he saw murder there. What the hell was it all about? he wondered.

He thought he could call Cole's bluff if he could appear unperturbed. He would have liked to turn his back on Cole and casually dress himself. But he couldn't turn his back.

He looked at the shirt he held as if it had his whole attention. Shaking it, he found a sleeve. Pretending to ignore Cole, he started to slip the hand that held the Remington through the sleeve. Cole fired.

Todd felt the slug snatch at the shirt. He felt himself wince.

" 'Let it lie,' I said," Cole growled.

Todd knew the sudden fear that perhaps Cole wasn't buffing. Damn him, he thought. His hands were trying to shake. He swallowed hard and struggled to keep the hands steady as he continued the move he had begun. His body was tense, expecting another slug. One that would rack into him and slam him to hell.

But Cole didn't fire.

As Todd shrugged the shirt onto his shoulders and knew the scars were covered, he suddenly felt more at ease. Less vulnerable. Safe behind his mask. And certain now that Cole's gun was a bluff.

Turning his back to Cole, he set down the pistol and reached for his smallclothes. As he picked them up, he heard the creak of saddle leather. It told him Cole was dismounting. He straightened and glanced over his shoulder.

Cole was striding toward him.

Cole's free hand grabbed. The fingers clamped into the point of Todd's shoulder, wrenching. It was a vice grip that turned Todd against his will, almost stumbling him.

The muzzle of Cole's gum rammed into Todd's belly. It hit hard, jerking a grunt of pain from him.

In an instant of panic, he thought he had been wrong about Cole. Cole really would murder him. In the next instant, he wondered if it mattered. Perhaps it wouldn't answer the questions that had come to torment him, but it would put an end to them.

"Damn you!" Cole demanded. "Pay attention to me!"

"What do you want?" Todd's voice was level. Very calm.

"At first, I just figured to warn you off and send you back to town without them fancy breeches of yours. But now I got a notion to send you back without your guts."

"And be hanged for it?" Todd asked.

"Yes!"

"Then, go ahead."

Cole stared at him. Cole's face was very close to his. It was an intimidating closeness. One that could work in either direction. Todd used it, holding his eyes on Cole's. A cold, steady, insistent gaze. He knew he could break the tension simply by asking what the hell this was all about. He wanted to know. But the man who moved first, the one who shifted his gaze or spoke a word, would be yielding to the other. And Todd's urge to defy Cole was too strong. No mattter how wise it might be to give in, Todd couldn't do it. He didn't understand that. He had always been able to change color like a chameleon, to play the coward if it would profit him. But not now.

His gaze held Cole's, icy and taut.

Cole blinked. His face was reddening. His lips twitched. Slowly he back-stepped. His hand slid away from Todd's shoulder. The pressure of the gun against Todd's body eased.

Todd couldn't help glancing down at the gun. He saw the hammer under Cole's thumb. It wasn't cocked. Cole's talk of killing had been bluff after all.

Todd felt a sudden relief, and realized he wasn't as ready to die yet as he had thought.

There was puzzlement in Cole's voice. "You don't scare so easy today."

I'm not playing the same role today, Todd thought. He wondered what role he was playing. There was no planning behind his words. He had slipped out of the character he was supposed to be. He didn't know who he was. He heard himself answer Cole, "Should I?"

"I thought you would. When I threw down on you at the dam yesterday, you squirmed plenty." Cole was frowning, bewildered by the difference between his expectations for this encounter and the actuality. He spoke of the expectations. "Hell, you're nothing but a damned highfalutin, lace-drawers dude. You ain't got the guts to stand up to me."

Todd gave a snorting laugh. His smallclothes were still in his hand.

Calmly, he stepped away from the gun and continued dressing himself. With his trousers on, he collected his collar and cravat. He buttoned the collar into place, then deftly tied the cravat.

Cole was watching him as if he were undergoing a mysterious transformation, becoming once again the man that Cole had cowed yesterday at the dam. Still angry, again defiant, Cole said, "You wear a damned fop's duds and you carry a damned fop's gun."

Dressed, Todd felt the transformation himself. He felt himself in the role of a gentleman again. He said quietly, "If you insist, I shall consider myself properly insulted."

"Huh?"

Todd picked up his coat and hunted his cardcase out of a pocket. He flipped it open, took out a card, and held it toward Cole. He wondered what the hell he would do if Cole accepted it. "Have your friend call on me at the hotel in the morning."

Puzzled, Cole scowled suspiciously at the card. It took him a moment to figure out what Todd had in mind. Incredulously he said, "A duel?"

"If you insist," Todd answered.

Cole kept gazing at the card. He looked as if he were trying to stare down a rattlesnake. He didn't reach out for the card. Instead he admitted slowly, "I don't *want* to kill you."

He sounded as if he were certain he could. Irked, Todd said, "Do you think you could?"

"You think I couldn't?"

"It's been tried."

That stirred Cole's curiosity. "That where you got that bullet scar?"

"Yes."

"The other man?"

"He didn't die. But he lost an arm."

"If neither of you died, who won the duel?"

A corner of Todd's mouth quirked. "Nobody wins a duel. Have you ever killed a man, Mister McRae?"

"I've been in a few shooting scrapes."

"Have you ever faced a man on the field? Have you ever stood through the count with your pistol at your side, waiting to raise and fire it at a man? Waiting for him to raise his pistol and try his damnedest to kill you?"

Reluctant to make the admission, Cole shook his head. He looked at the card Todd still held toward him. He still didn't take it.

"The choice is yours," Todd said. "But it is customary for gentlemen to try to settle matters without bloodshed. Sometimes there are very simple misunderstandings—"

"This is no damned misunderstanding!" Cole was suddenly reminded of his reason for being there. The anger flared hot in his eyes. "I was watching from inside the house. I seen you looking at her. I know that look. I know what you've been thinking and you damned better stay away from her!"

Todd understood. And didn't understand. Frowning, he said, "Your sister?"

"My sister is a fine woman! A clean, decent woman! No damned soft-talking city-bred son of a bitch is going to roll my sister in the hay and then forget her!"

Todd gave a shake of his head. He ran his fingers through

his hair as he ran Cole's words through his mind. Licking his lips, he asked, "What the hell gave you that idea?"

"I seen you look at her like a damned stud horse. I know what your kind wants!"

"My kind?"

Cole nodded.

"What makes you so certain that my intentions are dishonorable?" Todd asked.

Cole still had the big revolver in his hand. He made an angry gesture with it. "Fancy duds. Fancy talk. It's all a damned fancy front and so rotten inside that the buzzards wouldn't touch your carcass."

For a fearful instant, Todd thought Cole had learned the truth somehow.

But Cole went on, "You're the same cut as that bastard Edmund, and you look at her the same way. Hell, I should have killed him!"

Todd understood then that it was an old hatred of Don Edmund that was spilling over onto him because of similarities in the roles they played.

"I should kill you!" Cole added fiercely.

Without knowing it, Todd nodded. Cole was right. Todd wanted Asia McRae. But, dammit, he was in no position to have intentions toward her, honorable or otherwise. He was in no position to do anything except what Millard Samson was paying him to do. And in the end, he would hurt her.

Sidestepping, he walked past Cole. He could sense Cole's burning eyes on his back as he jerked loose the reins and stepped up onto his horse.

"Hey!" Cole shouted. "I'm not through with you yet!"

Todd felt himself tense, anticipating a bullet in his back. Dammit, he didn't want to die. He didn't want to keep going in the direction he was heading either. But what alternatives were there?

He heeled the horse toward the dark defile that led away from the Indian spring.

Cole didn't fire.

CHAPTER 11

Todd eased open his eyes, then slammed them shut again. Brilliant sunlight blazed into the hotel room. Very cautiously, he squinted through his lashes. It looked to be late morning. He had drunk himself to sleep in the rocker.

His sleep had been deep. His head ached now, and his eyes were gummy. His throat felt thick and very dry. The bottle was still in his lap, and there was still whiskey in it. He took enough of a drink to cut the scum in his mouth, then hoisted himself out of the chair. His legs didn't want to take his weight. His head tottered atop his neck. His shoulders were still wearily stiff. A lot of good that night's sleep had done.

Confronting himself in the mirror, he shook his head in disgusted despair. The image that looked back at him had a slack mockery of a face with red, haggard eyes. His clothes looked like they had been slept in. Of course.

It would take a long, hot bath and a shave, a fresh shirt and smallclothes, and a lot of black coffee to turn that image into the respectable James Reynard Todd. He would have preferred the coffee first, but a gentleman had to keep up appearances above all else. He couldn't sit in a public place very long looking like this. So it was the barbershop first and then the coffee.

As he stepped out of the hotel lobby, he saw people bunched along the walk in little clusters, their heads together and their voices an excited murmur. There was tension in the air, a sense of something very important having happened. An overt act in the war that Don Edmund was trying to start? he wondered. He hoped not. He didn't want the McRaes suffering.

There were several men in the barbershop, gabbling together. Todd's entrance brought sudden silence. Eyes turned toward him, curious and appraising and distrustful of strangers.

The barber didn't consider Todd exactly a stranger. Beaming with the pleasure of bearing big news, waving his razor in excitement, he said, "Mr. Todd! Did you hear about the killing?"

"No."

"It's Don Edmund! I think you met him in here the first time you came in. He's the editor of the newspaper—"

"He *was* the editor," the man in the chair interrupted. "He ain't any more."

The men laughed. It was tense, nervous laughter.

"What happened to him?" Todd asked, trying to sound only casually interested.

The barber picked up the story. "They found his body early this morning, down near the Stick River Bridge. Josh Waite found him. He'd been shot. In the back!"

The men were watching Todd closely, waiting for his reaction. They seemed to expect the fancy-pants dude to be shocked, perhaps to swoon away.

Todd gave an appalled shake of his head. "Terrible!"

"First killing we've had in these parts in a piece of time," one man admitted. He seemed uncertain whether to be proud or embarrassed by the admission.

The barber added, "This wasn't ever one of those rip-roaring hell towns you hear about. Not since I been here. This had always been a real peaceable place."

"There was the time Billy Westphal and Long Will Long got into that ruckus over Tom Schneider's daughter—" a man began.

Todd wasn't interested in that. He asked, "Have they apprehended the murderer?"

"Not yet," the barber said. "But they've got *lots* of suspects."

There was another murmur of laughter, with a forced, uncomfortable sound to it, as if each man felt obligated to express amusement.

"Edmund had enemies?" Todd said.

The barber grinned. "Barrels of them."

"I say it was Cole McRae who done it," the man in the chair volunteered. He scanned the group around him. "You all seen how he lit into Edmund the other day. He's got a temper on him like a grizzly bear, that boy."

"He's feisty, all right," one of the others said. "But he ain't the kind to go bushwhacking a man in the back."

Another countered, "You get riled up enough, you'll shoot at whatever part of a feller as makes a target for you."

They fell to arguing it among themselves.

Todd stood silently considering. After that encounter at the Indian spring yesterday, he could imagine Cole McRae angry enough to kill a man. But he couldn't see Cole waylaying his victim, shooting him in the back.

The law might disagree.

And if Cole were accused, it could complicate Todd's situation, perhaps interfere with the swindle.

From the way these men were talking, Todd thought Cole might very well be accused.

He ran a hand into his pocket, aware of the money there. It was enough to get him out of Stick City. Not enough to stake him to a new life. He thought he had damned well better get this deal completed quickly.

Catching the barber's attention, he asked for a hot bath.

He didn't linger long in the bath. Not nearly as long as he would have liked. When he came out, he found a man in the chair. He would have to wait for his shave.

He was sitting studying his plan, looking for shortcuts, when the *Sentinel* composer, Andy Groseille, appeared in the doorway.

"Take a seat, Andy," the barber called to him. "I got another one ahead of you."

"'Fraid not," Groseille answered. His eyes were bright, his face flushed. He looked full of secrets. Very pleasant secrets.

He didn't look at all like a man concerned with the murder of a close associate. He glanced at Todd and told the barber, "I came to take him away from you."

Todd lifted a brow at Groseille.

"There's something I want to show you, Mr. Todd. Over in the shop," Groseille said.

"I haven't the time now," Todd answered. "I'll stop by later."

"You'd better come now. It's about a *fox*." Groseille emphasized the word. "In France."

Todd blinked. His eyes on Groseille narrowed. There was question in them.

Groseille nodded.

Todd's throat was suddenly very dry. Swallowing hard, he rose. He followed Groseille onto the walk, then faced him and asked, "What's this all about?"

"I'll show you at the shop," Groseille said, and he grinned.

All along the street, shop doors stood open, hopeful of some small breeze. All except the door to the *Sentinel* office. It was locked. Groseille unlocked it, let Todd in, then locked it again. The office was an oven, the air thick and strong with the scent of printer's ink. The high sun glowed through the dirty skylight overhead, casting dusty shadows around the big press. Groseille led Todd past the counter and over to the press.

A column of type was locked up in the frame on the bed. Above the text type was a two-column head and an engraving. Groseille inked the form and put a proof sheet on it. As he grabbed the lever of the press, he told Todd cheerily, "We printers call this the 'devil's tail.'"

He twisted the devil's tail, and the platen dropped onto the paper with a groan. He released it and the counterweight pulled the platen up again. The press sighed. Groseille took the paper by the corner and peeled it off the type carefully. He held it out to Todd. "Be careful. The ink's wet. Don't get it on you. It's damned hard to get it off."

Todd accepted the proof sheet. The two-column head read:

NOTORIOUS SWINDLER IN STICK CITY. The story under it was a detailed account of the affair in Paris, no more accurate than newspaper stories usually were, but precise enough. The engraving was a simple line drawing, just a man's face. Todd's face.

"A good likeness, don't you think?" Groseille said proudly.

Todd nodded. It was a remarkably good likeness. He licked his lips, then asked, "Your work?"

"Sure. I'm a damned good artist. I studied in Paris for three years. I would have been famous. Rich. But my father died and there was no more money for my studies. I had to come home and work to support my mother and sisters. You don't remember me, but we did meet in Paris. At Lorena Chantre's salon. You know, you've aged quite a bit since then. I almost didn't recognize you."

"I've had time to age," Todd mumbled. He remembered those salons. There had always been a clutter of strangers. Lorena Chantre fancied herself a patroness of the arts. Her salons were open to students and drifters. Penniless young people not worthy of a self-respecting swindler's attention. At least Todd hadn't noticed the males. The females had been another matter. He didn't recall Groseille's face at all. He said, "You remember me?"

"I had a young lady in my company when I went to the salon. She didn't leave with me. She stayed with you. I resented that. Your arrest delighted me. I followed every detail, every bit of gossip that I could pick up."

Todd's eyes were still on the proof sheet. He said, "You have this set in type. Do you intended to print it?"

"Don was planning to. It was to be the front-page story in a special edition." Groseille's voice hooked upward, leaving an implication unspoken.

"But you don't?"

"It depends."

"Money?"

Groseille grinned.

"How much?" Todd asked.

"I'm not greedy. I'll settle for half of whatever you take here. And don't think you can trick me into accepting less. In a place like this, word gets around. I'll know how much you've got the same day it's in your hand."

Todd grunted. Samson had demanded half before he would finance the swindle. Now Groseille wanted half. That didn't leave Todd a hell of a lot.

Groseille added, "Or would you rather hang?"

"Hang?"

"You knew that Don was onto you, didn't you? Why else would you kill him?"

"*What!*"

"Don't try me, Fox. Don was following you around. He wanted to get a line on the swindle you planned here. He hoped he could include that in his special edition. You spotted him and realized he was onto you. Or he slipped up somehow and gave himself away. You killed him. And I know it."

"If I killed Don Edmund to keep him quiet," Todd said softly, "what's to stop me from doing the same to you?"

Groseille grinned again. "I set this type last night. This morning, when I heard about Don, I came and pulled proofs. Lots of them. I put each one into an envelope addressed to a newspaper in a big city. New York and Boston and New Orleans and Denver, places like that. I took the original copy in Don's handwriting—I only told him what I knew about you and he wrote the story—and I put that in an envelope addressed to the sheriff in Dadeston. Right now they're all together in a nice safe place where you could never find them. No one will touch them. Not unless something should happen to me. If I died, those envelopes would all be mailed. If I were murdered the way Don was, the people who read that story would begin to wonder. You *know* what they'd wonder, don't you?"

Todd nodded.

"You wouldn't want anything to happen to me, Mr. Todd," Groseille said.

"No," Todd agreed. His chest felt tight, his throat

cramped. He didn't doubt the story would look like motive
for murder. People who had been made fools of were quick to
convict. The story alone, even without murder, would be
enough to start lynch talk.

He saw the glitter in Groseille's eyes and said, "You've chosen the wrong profession, Mr. Groseille. You should be in my
line."

"Not me. I wouldn't like prison. I intend to go back to
Paris. Take up my art studies again."

"About these envelopes? You'll turn them over to me when
I give you the money?"

"They'll stay where they are until you're long gone. When
I'm ready to leave for France, I'll burn them."

"How can I be certain of that? How can I know you won't
follow me and do this again?"

"You have my word."

Todd hesitated. There was no point in saying what he was
thinking. But he had damned little confidence in Groseille's
word.

Instead he asked, "Suppose I fail here. It could happen."

"Don't let it happen, Mr. Fox."

"I'd appreciate it if you would address me as 'Todd' while
I'm here."

"Certainly." Groseille smiled.

Todd was still holding the proof. He gestured toward the
frame on the press. "What about that?"

"I'll break it up. I can always set it again."

"Now?"

Obligingly, Groseille opened the form while Todd
watched. He pied the type thoroughly and tucked the engraving away on a shelf. As he wiped his ink-stained hands, he
asked, "Satisfied?"

Todd was far from satisfied. He tapped a finger on the
proof sheet. "Are there any more of these?"

"Just that and the ones I told you about, the ones all sealed
in envelopes and stored in a safe place."

"All right." Todd could see no reason for Groseille to lie

about that. He started to crumple the sheet and toss it into the waste. But he thought better of it. Folding the sheet carefully, the inky side in, he tucked it into a vest pocket.

Groseille unlocked the door to let him out. "Have a good day, Mr. Fox—uh—Todd."

"Sure," Todd muttered, walking away. Outside, he took a deep breath. But it didn't ease the cramp in his chest. He was in a box. A goddamned coffin, with the lid nailed on. There was no way out.

What he needed, he decided, was a good, stiff drink.

CHAPTER 12

Standing at the bar, gazing into the glass he held, Todd told himself this was no good. Whiskey wasn't the answer. The situation was too precarious. If he wasn't careful, he could drink himself back into prison—or into a grave.

He glanced at the gold ring on his left hand. He had bought it for insurance. It was something he could sell if he had to run suddenly. But now he coudn't run. Not with Groseille ready to send out that story on his heels. The story and the picture. A very distinctive face.

He looked at the face reflected in the back-bar mirror. Groseille had done a damned good likeness.

There was only one way. Get his hands on Amos McRae's money. Pay off Samson and Groseille. He would be left with nothing but the gold ring. And his hide in one piece. At least he would have a chance to escape. Try again somewhere, somehow. First he had to take the money from Amos McRae.

He finished the drink and turned his back on the bar.

The hotel dining room was open now. He had missed dinner yesterday and he couldn't remember any supper. He didn't feel hungry but he knew he would have to eat something.

The meal he ordered was light and simple. He idled over it, forcing down each mouthful. When he had finally finished, he sat with a cup of coffee, contemplating the meeting he planned with the McRaes. The timing was crucial. He had to pull it off today, tomorrow at the latest.

What he needed, he decided, was another drink.

The saloon was quiet this early in the day. The bartender was excited about the murder of Don Edmund. He wanted to

discuss it with someone. There was no one in the saloon but
Todd. And Todd didn't want to talk. He ordered his drink
and rudely rebuffed the bartender's attempted conversation.
At last the bartender withdrew to the far end of the bar and
set in to sullenly wiping glasses.

Todd tasted his drink and told himself it was the last one
he would order today. When this glass was empty, he would
get on with his business.

He didn't look up when the squeal of the batwings told
him someone was coming. He supposed it was simply another
customer. The touch on his sleeve startled him. It was a light
touch, but not an accidental one. A voice close at his back
said, "Mr. Todd?"

He turned and found himself facing a stranger, a stocky,
graying man in a baggy business suit. The suit coat was unbuttoned, hanging open to show the star pinned to the man's
vest. It was a plain, cheap star that had been polished until its
domed center gleamed, but there was tarnish on the edges
and in the engraved lettering, DEPUTY SHERIFF. It looked as
if it had been gotten out and buffed up for a special occasion.

For a murder investigation, Todd thought as he looked
from the star to the face of the man wearing it. The deputy's
Stetson was pushed to the back of his head, showing a pallid
forehead darkening into a sun-browned, weather-beaten jaw.
The face of a man who spent much of his time out of doors.
There were lines of laughter around the mouth, and of weariness around the eyes. But the eyes themselves were quick and
sharp. Too sharp. This man wouldn't be easy to bluff.

Todd looked at him in question.

"You're Mr. James R. Todd, staying at the hotel here?" the
deputy asked, already knowing the answer.

"At your service, sir," Todd said, trying to find the feel of
his role, hoping he sounded like the man he was supposed to
be.

"I'm Charlie Horne, deputy at this end of the county. I'd
be obliged if I could have a palaver with you, Mr. Todd."

"Is something wrong?"

Horne gave a significant glance toward the bartender, who was sidling nearer, alert to overhear. He suggested, "Why don't we go up to your room to talk?"

Todd didn't like it. Not at all. But at least the deputy wasn't suggesting they talk at the local jailhouse. Nodding, Todd set a coin by his glass, which still held a good finger of whiskey.

"You want to finish your drink?" Horne said pleasantly.

"No."

As they walked toward the door, Horne's hand was on Todd's arm. It pressured him just slightly, just enough for him to feel it. Just enough for him to be damned uncomfortable about it.

The hotel room was just as Todd had left it. The bedclothes were rumpled and the whiskey bottle lay on the floor beside the chair. The luggage was all tucked away, out of sight under the bed. Horne's quick glance took in the details.

Todd looked around. He could see nothing that he couldn't explain. He hoped Horne didn't ask to examine his luggage. He felt an urge to pick up the whiskey bottle, set it straight, make up the mussed bed, make the room all neat and proper.

Trying to order his thoughts, to keep his role neat and proper, he faced Horne. His tone was curious, nothing more. "You wanted to talk to me, sir?"

Horne gave a sigh. "Mind if I set? My feet don't take so kindly to boots as they used to."

"Please do." Todd indicated the chair.

Horne slumped into it and stretched his legs out in front of him. His boots were the cowboy kind, high-heeled and sharply pointed at the toe. Probably too small. They were well-worn, rubbed rough where spur straps had crossed them. The heels were worn askew with too much walking. They were boots that had been around.

Horne looked as if he had been around.

"I hear you're in town to buy land, Mr. Todd," he said.

It was meant as a question, but it wasn't phrased as one. Todd didn't offer a reply.

"Are you?" Horne asked.

"If you'll excuse me, sir," Todd said. "I would like to know your reason for asking."

"Do you mind saying?"

"I prefer to keep my business affairs private."

Horne smiled. It was a pleasant smile. He seemed very agreeable, not at all suspicious. Todd didn't trust him. "There ain't much a man can keep private in parts like these," Horne said. "Folks around here ain't got much to talk about. When something comes along, they talk about it a lot. Rumors fly every which way. Word has it that you want to buy that old Indian spring up in the badlands off Amos McRae."

He paused for a reply. But he hadn't put it to Todd as a question. Again, Todd offered no response.

Horne went on. "It puzzles a body why a gentleman like yourself, Mr. Todd, would want a worthless section like that."

"Do you believe I have some nefarious purpose?"

"Don't seem likely," Horne allowed. "All that talk about gold up there, it just ain't so. Every young buck ever been within a hundred miles of Stick City has sneaked up there and had him a hunt for it. None of them found it. I hunted it myself quite a piece back. Didn't find a damn thing. Amos says there just ain't no gold in there. I say Amos is right."

Todd nodded in agreement.

Horne sighed. His eyes shifted around the room and returned to Todd's face. "You knew Donald Edmund well, did you, Mr. Todd?"

"No. I'm afraid I didn't know Mr. Edmund at all."

"Seems you and him and Andy Groseille were all drinking together not long after you got into town."

"Yes. Mr. Edmund did introduce himself to me. We chatted briefly. As a newspaperman, Mr. Edmund seemed interested in my presence here."

"How did he come to follow you out of town?"

"Sir?"

"You know when you went riding he was following you, didn't you? As I figure it"—Horne started counting on his fingers—"you come into town and met him in the barbershop right off. A little later that afternoon, you went over to the newspaper office and seen him. Next day, you hired a horse and went riding and Edmund followed along after you. That night, you and him drank together. Next morning, you went riding again and he followed you again. That afternoon some body shot him in the back and left him dead under the bridge. When was the last time you seen him, Mr. Todd?"

Todd licked his lips. He said, "I was aware that someone was behind me on the trail out to the Pitchfork ranch. I was not aware that it was Mr. Edmund following me. The last time I knowingly saw him was that evening in the saloon, when he and Mr. Groseille stopped at my table. As I said, he simply inquired as to what brought me to Stick City."

"You tell him?"

"No. I don't care to make my business affairs public."

Horne pursed his face. "Why you reckon he'd go around following you that way?"

With a shrug, Todd suggested, "He was looking for news. Perhaps he hoped I would lead him to some."

"Might be," Horne said. He hefted himself out of the chair, wincing slightly as he took his weight on his feet. "Don Edmund was that kind, nosy as hell. Aways turning over rocks and poking into closets." Chuckling, he added, "Hiding in a few closets, too."

"Perhaps you would find motive for murder around those closets," Todd said.

"A jealous lover or husband, you mean? I been thinking about that." Horne walked to the door. He put a hand on the knob. Pausing, he looked back. "By the way, Mr. Todd, there's one more reason I can think of besides gold why a man might want that old Indian spring."

"What?"

"Might be he's got a mind to dam it up and cut off a lot of water that folks around here depend on during the dry spells.

Might be he figured on selling the water. Or running folk out of business and picking up their land cheap. Or some damn thing like that. Might be, if Don Edmund found out such a thing, a man would kill him just to keep him quiet about it."

"Sir!" Todd said indignantly.

"Much obliged for your co-operation, Mr. Todd." Horne smiled. He walked out, closing the door behind him.

Todd scowled at the door. Turning, he picked up the bottle. He looked at the short swallow of whiskey left in it. With a shake of his head, he put the bottle on the commode.

First Groseille, now this. What the hell would the Colonel have done in a situation like this? Found yet another swindle, Todd supposed. One that would let him pay off Samson and Groseille and still ride out with his own pockets full. The Colonel had been a master at pulling switches, covering his bets, recouping his losses. Except for that one, last time when it all went sour for him. Just as sour as this job looked now.

Thinking of the press proof, Todd pulled it from his pocket and unfolded it. The ink had smeared. The words were blurred and the face in the engraving seemed to be lifting its brows in question. He set the paper in the basin on the commode, lit a match, and held it to one corner.

He stood watching as the flame spread over the type and ate through the face. Then it was all gone. Nothing remained but ashes.

CHAPTER 13

Amos McRae was sitting in a rocker on the veranda, his lame leg outstretched on an upended nail keg. As Todd rode into the yard, Amos called to him, "Step down and set. Excuse me for not getting up. This old leg's bothering me." Hopefully he added, "It always gives me trouble when there's a hard rain coming."

Todd glanced at the sky. There were a few wisps of cloud. They were the thin, useless kind that offered no promise at all.

"Sarah," Amos shouted at the house, "Mr. Todd's here!"

Dismounting, Todd looped his reins around the hitch rail and started up the steps.

Sarah bobbed out the door to greet him. She beamed at him. "It's good to see you, Mr. Todd! You'll stay for supper, won't you? Now, I won't take no for an answer. It's no trouble at all."

Amos grinned. "You better say yes, Mr. Todd. The way you went rushing off yesterday upset the womenfolk. They had a lot of fancies planned for you. It ain't too often they get company to set the table for."

"The way you hurried off yesterday, I was afraid something was wrong," Sarah said.

Todd felt himself responding to her smile and concern. He felt himself hating what he must do here. He had to swallow and clear his throat before he could reply. "I regret my hasty departure, madame, but it was a pressing business matter. I was enjoying your hospitality so much that I almost forgot about it completely."

"Asia said you seemed like something was worrying you," Sarah told him. "I hope it wasn't anything serious."

Gravely, he said, "I'm afraid something serious has come up."

"Oh?" Amos frowned at him. "Something about the spa?"

"You remember I told you I had a business partner?"

"Yeah?"

"I received a message today that he's dead."

"Oh, heavens!" Sarah said. "How terrible! I hope this doesn't mean you'll be leaving Stick City!"

"I'm afraid it does."

She looked off at the horizon. "Asia's out riding. She'll be back soon, I'm sure. She'll be so disappointed! You're not leaving now, are you? Not this minute? You can stay for supper, can't you?"

Todd wasn't sure he wanted to see Asia again. But he didn't want to leave without seeing her again. But—hell—there wasn't any way he could leave until his business here was done. He would have to face Asia.

"It would be my pleasure, madame. It would give me one more happy memory of your hospitality here to take back with me."

Sarah beamed again. Wiping her hands on her apron, she said, "If you men will excuse me, I've got things to tend in the kitchen. Amos, would you send a man to find Asia and fetch her home?"

"I'll send one. Can't promise he'll find her. You know how that girl is."

"Likely she's up to the spring. She likes to ride up that way."

Amos nodded, and Sarah scurried into the house. Amos gave a shout that brought the stable boy from the barn. He told the boy to tend Todd's horse, then find Asia if he could. When the boy was gone, Amos turned to Todd again. "Your friend's death is gonna affect your plans here, ain't it?"

"I'm afraid so. You know, my partner was to put up over half of the initial capital investment."

Amos nodded.

Todd continued, "Unfortunately, we hadn't consummated the arrangement. It was a gentleman's agreement. There was no contract, and no cash had changed hands. Now he has died intestate. He has children by a first wife, and more by a second wife. They bicker. There will be trouble. The estate will most probably be tied up in the courts for months. Possibly years. There is no hope now of any of his money coming into the project. And I am in no position at the moment to put up the entire hundred thousand myself."

"Can't you find somebody else to come into it with you?" Amos asked. "If this spa thing is as good a deal as you say it is, you shouldn't have any trouble getting more backing."

Todd drew breath and sighed. "There is the matter of time. We had a meeting with the officers of the railroad scheduled in two weeks. I had intended to telegraph my partner that I had completed arrangements here and give him the necessary details. He was to make a presentation to the railroad. Now, if I could somehow raise the money, I would have to make the presentation myself. It will take me better than a week to get back to New York. It would be impossible for me to find another investor who could put sixty thousand dollars cash in my hand in the few days I would have before the meeting."

"Can't you postpone the meeting?"

"This is a very delicately balanced situation, sir. There are other localities bidding for spur lines and offering various reasons for the railroad to build to them. There are towns willing to issue bonds and offer financial incentives." Todd gave a twist to the corner of his mouth, implying even more than he said. "I have certain influence, and if I could go before the board with my project in hand, already capitalized and the land optioned, I would have the spur line, no question. But if I started stalling, putting the railroad off—well, there are other men with influence. You understand?"

Amos nodded thoughtfully and asked, "What do you have in mind to do now?"

Todd shrugged. "There isn't anything I can do. My forty thousand isn't enough. I'll just have to forget this project and find another investment for myself."

"But what about us?" Amos hefted himself to his feet and faced Todd. "What about Stick City? We *need* that railroad spur."

"There is very little I can do without the spa to offer the railroad as incentive." Todd shaped an expression of regret and embarrassment. "However, if you would draw up a prospectus on what Stick City has to offer, giving good reason why a railroad spur should be built here, I shall gladly present it for you. I shall use my influence in your behalf. But I can hardly promise results."

"Without the spa, they ain't likely to come here?"

"No."

"Hell," Amos muttered. He limped to the edge of the veranda and looked at the sky. Even the thin wisps of cloud were disappearing. "Hell."

"I'm extremely sorry," Todd said. "But there just isn't anything more I can do. Not without a partner who can put up sixty thousand in cash."

Amos started for the door. "Come into the house, Mr. Todd. I'd like a drink."

Todd followed Amos into the parlor and settled into the easy chair. When Amos offered him a drink, Todd forced himself to decline. He had drunk too much already that day. One now could easily lead to another, then another. And this was the critical moment. He had to carry this through now without a slip.

Amos poured a brandy for himself, and sat down across from Todd. He took a swallow, then looked at Todd. It was a deep, searching look. "You tell me about this spa again."

"Sir?"

"Tell me all about it, like you hadn't ever told me any of it before. Tell me what the railroad has promised you. Tell me *all* about it."

"I don't see the point," Todd said, lying.

"Just tell me," Amos insisted.

Todd went through the story with Amos listening intently, picking at details. Amos managed to find questions Todd had failed to anticipate. But Todd found answers.

They were still discussing it when Cole came into the house. He started at the sight of Todd. Todd smiled at him.

"Cole, boy," Amos said, rising. "I want to talk to you. Excuse us a minute, Mr. Todd."

"Certainly."

Amos took Cole onto the veranda. Todd could see them through the open window. He was tempted to move close enough to the window to listen. But he couldn't chance being caught at it. He sat tense, wanting the drink Amos had offered. He could have helped himself to it easily enough. But he didn't dare that either. Taut, he waited.

Asia rode up while Cole and Amos were on the veranda. She joined them and after a while their voices rose as if they argued.

Todd heard Asia protest, "Cole, don't make a fool of yourself!"

"Better for me to do it than have the whole bunch of us all do it!" Cole answered. A moment later, he came slamming into the parlor, with Asia and Amos trailing after him.

Rising, Todd greeted Asia.

Before she could reply, Cole was demanding, "Todd, what proof have we got that all these things you've been telling us are true? How do we know you're not chousing us around the barn?"

Stiffly, Todd said, "You have my word, sir."

"Please, Mr. Todd," Asia said, "don't be offended. Cole is just—just—hasty."

"He's hotheaded," Amos said. "He goes off half-cocked. Thing is, he does kinda have a point there. I don't mean you any offense, Mr. Todd, but the fact is, all we've got is your word."

Todd gave the appearance of suppressing anger. His eyes met Asia's for an instant. In that instant, he felt ashamed. He fought the feeling aside. Concentrating on being James R. Todd, a gentleman, he faced Amos. "It is a matter of honor, sir. But under the circumstances, I cannot see that the question should be of any concern to you. The matter is closed. I shall be leaving on the coach Saturday."

Asia gave a small shake of her head. A protesting gesture she wasn't aware she made.

"Maybe it ain't closed," Amos said. He waved a hand to shush Cole. "Do you *want* to close it, Mr. Todd? Or would you sooner go on through with it just the way you got it all planned?"

Todd lifted his brows. "Without the necessary capital, I cannot possibly go through with it as planned."

"Maybe you'll get the capital."

"Where?"

"Tell me, if I could put sixty thousand dollars cash in your hand, would you want to go through with it just like you told me about it all?"

"Of course. I have already made a personal investment. I have made an extremely difficult trip out here. And I've undergone some trying experiences since I arrived." Todd darted a significant look at Cole. "I am hardly happy about writing all that off as a loss, a complete waste."

Slowly, still uncertain, Amos admitted, "Maybe I could raise the money."

"We'd have to go into debt for it," Cole protested. "Dammit, Pa, we can't go into debt in times like these. We're losing cattle to the drought now. We could go broke. We might lose the whole shebang."

"We'll get rain," Amos answered. "Maybe not today, but it'll come. Grass'll grow and the beef'll get fat again."

"And they could stay fat," Asia added, "if we didn't have to walk all the meat off them getting them to the railhead."

"But we'd be gambling everything we got on *his* word." Cole gave a jerk of his head toward Todd.

Todd said nothing. He had arguments. He could use them

if it became necessary. But it was far better to let them convince themselves.

"Mr. Todd's word is good enough for me," Asia said. She took a small step that put her facing her father and brother. It brought her near to Todd's side, as if she had chosen to stand with him against them.

"I've gambled before," Amos said, his voice still speculative. "I gambled coming out to this country. I gambled bringing in them Durhams. Every spring it's a gamble we'll get calves. A gamble we'll get rain. It's a gamble when we drive to the railroad. We're gambling we'll get the beef there and get a price for it. There's hardly anything in life that ain't a gamble."

"I don't like it," Cole grumbled.

Asia glared at him. "I've seen you gamble often enough, Cole McRae! Is it the gamble that worries you, or is it just that you dislike Mr. Todd?"

He narrowed his eyes at her. "I didn't say that."

"You didn't have to say it. Ever since he came here you've been acting as if he were some kind of—of—*thief* or something!"

"Hell, sis!"

"She's right about that," Amos told his son. "You got something in particular against Mr. Todd, boy?"

"I don't like the way he dresses," Cole mumbled.

Todd allowed himself a comment. "I am hardly overawed by the magnificence of your attire."

"Hell," Cole said again. He was outnumbered and he knew it. "Pa, it's your ranch. You do whatever you want with it. Only, you just take care for the womenfolk, that's all!"

Wheeling, he stalked out.

Amos lifted a brow at Asia.

Her face reddened. Muttering something unintelligible, she turned and hurried toward the kitchen.

"So that's it," Amos said to himself.

"May I ask what, sir?" Todd said.

Amos went to the sideboard and poured himself another

brandy. Lowering himself into a chair, he told Todd, "Sit down."

When Todd had settled across from him, Amos began, "Cole's rankled. He's been rankled a long piece now. The thing is, he had this girl friend. A little girl who worked as housemaid for Millard Samson and his missus—"

"The girl there now?"

"No, not her. The girl who worked there before her. Name of Edith Soroki. Pretty little thing. Cole got all calf-eyed over her. Had himself a notion to marry her. Only, it turned out that Don Edmund was hiding his horse in the bushes over to the Samson place. Then, one day, Edith drank down a whole bottle of laudanum. Killed herself. They found out afterward that she was—uh—in the family way."

"For Edmund?"

"Reckon so. Cole went kinda loco. He wanted to kill Edmund."

Todd looked up sharply, wondering if Cole had finally carried his grudge to its conclusion. Perhaps there was murder in Cole McRae.

"We got him calmed down after a while," Amos was saying. "But he ain't never really got over it. When you come along dressing fancy like Edmund and talking fancy like him, I guess Cole figured you and him were cut from the same cloth. When you started getting friendly with Asia, and her with you, he—well—Edmund give Asia a hard time once, and I reckon Cole just figured—you understand me, Mr. Todd?"

Todd nodded.

"I'm much obliged that you do," Amos said with a sigh. He finished off his drink, then leaned back in his chair and eyed Todd. "Fact is, I like you myself. So do the womenfolk. I hate to go against Cole, but I figure he just ain't seeing this matter straight."

"Sir?"

"Mr. Todd, you strike me as an honest man, and this proposition you've offered us is a good one. Stick City needs that damned railroad. It looks to me like there's only one way to get it here now. It looks like I'll have to raise your sixty thousand for you. I'll have to mortgage the ranch to do it, but I reckon it's worth it."

"Yes, sir." The words slipped in a half whisper through Todd's lips. Amos McRae had taken the bait and was hooked. But Todd felt no relief, none of the pleasure and excitement he had known in the past. This was a stale, sour game. If there had been any other way out, he would have turned his back on it.

But there was no other way. Samson and Groseille had him boxed in.

With effort, he moved on to the next play. "I would have to have the money, either cash or a draft on a reputable bank, by Saturday. I absolutely have to be on the coach Saturday."

"Let's see. Today is Thursday." Amos frowned and gave a shake of his head. "No way I could get into Dadeston before the bank closes tomorrow. Even if I roused up the banker at his home and got him to talk business then and there, I couldn't be back with the money before Saturday night."

"The coach leaves at noon," Todd said.

Amos nodded. He sat a long moment deep in thought. At last he said, "I reckon there's only one way. I'll have to do business with Millard Samson. I'll go in tomorrow morning first thing. See him."

"Are you certain he'll give you the money?" Todd asked, knowing the answer.

Amos nodded sadly. "He's been hungry to get this place away from me for years. He'll be real glad to take a mortgage on it."

CHAPTER 14

"Mr. Todd," Amos said. "My mind is made up and you've got my word. I'm going to do what I think is best. But I'm not happy about Cole feeling the way he does. If you'll excuse me a few minutes, I want to go talk to him some more."

"Of course," Todd said.

Amos started to swing his lame leg down from the footstool it rested on. It was obvious that the leg hurt him.

"Why don't you wait here?" Todd suggested. "I'll find him and tell him you want to speak to him."

"Obliged." Amos eased the leg back onto the footstool. "Likely he's hanging around the stable. That's where he does his brooding when he ain't out on the range. And I ain't heard him ride off."

"I'll find him."

Todd walked out onto the veranda. Standing in its shade, he scanned the yard. There was someone working in a corral near the stable, but it wasn't Cole. He hoped he could find Cole quickly. Get this all over with quickly.

When he stepped out of the shade, the sun-heat hit him, sucking sweat onto his forehead. He wiped at it and glanced at the sky.

With some good rains and the good grass they would bring, Amos might be able to save himself. He held mortgages on other ranches. If the men who owed him money could pay him, he might be able to pay back Samson. He would be out sixty thousand dollars, but he would still have his ranch. Samson wouldn't have beaten him.

But there wasn't a hint of a cloud in the blue inferno of the sky now. No promise that there would ever be rain again.

The man in the corral was cleaning the hoofs of a pregnant mare. Todd called to him, asking if he had seen Cole. He replied with a sharp jerk of his head toward the stable.

At the doorway, Todd halted. After the brightness of the sun, the dim interior of the big building seemed night dark. It took a moment for his eyes to adjust, for him to see the figure of a man perched on the top rail of a stall.

Cole had a Bull Durham sack in one hand. He shook tobacco into a creased paper, returned the sack to his pocket, then sealed the cigarette. From the deftness of his fingers, the job didn't require the close attention he appeared to be giving it.

Standing back-lit in the brilliant square of the doorway, Todd felt obvious. He was certain Cole had noticed him, so Cole was pointedly ignoring him.

He walked up as Cole mouthed the cigarette.

Unspeaking, Cole took a match from his hatband, struck it, and lit the cigarette. Very deliberately, he squeezed the flame of the match out between his thumb and forefinger. Then, at last, he looked at Todd.

"Your father would like to speak with you," Todd said.

"He wants to tell me he's going to mortgage this place and give you the money," Cole said grimly. It wasn't a question.

Todd nodded.

Cole slid down off the rail. He stood facing Todd. "I don't know why the hell he thinks he can trust you, but if he's wrong, you're going to be damned sorry you ever set foot on Pitchfork land."

I'm already sorry, Todd thought. He said, "I assure you—"

"You don't assure me of anything! Mister, before you stood up to me yesterday, I figured you were just a fool. A damned fop. But you got guts. I'll say that for you. Now I think you're a gambler, and I can't tell which side of the deck you're dealing off. If I'm wrong about you, I'll apologize. If I ain't, I'll kill you."

Impulsively, Todd said, "The way you killed Don Edmund?"

"Like hell! I never did that!"

"You wanted to."

"Sure. I'm real glad somebody did it. But if I'd of done it, I'd of done it to his face."

That was true, Todd thought.

"If the time comes, I'll face you," Cole was saying. "And I'll kill you."

Todd said, "Your father is waiting for you in the parlor."

"If the time comes—" Cole repeated. Turning, he stalked out of the stable.

A horse was watching from its stall. It was the mount Todd had ridden. He went to it, scratched at its cheek, and thought of riding out. He could saddle up, steal the horse, and be in another town before anyone realized he had run out.

But there were telegraphs in other towns, and lawmen, and prisons. There were newspapers that would pick up Andy Groseille's story, and print shops that would turn out reward posters with Groseille's excellent likeness on them. There were a damned lot of things that would follow a man all the way to hell.

He gave the horse a pat on the neck and walked back toward the house.

Cole and Amos would be talking in the parlor. Todd knew they wanted privacy. He seated himself on the veranda.

Gazing at the far horizon, he saw dust. A small, thin cloud of it traveling toward the ranch. A rider, he thought.

Soon the rider came in sight. It was a man on a squat, ugly bay horse. Todd winced as he recognized the deputy, Charlie Horne.

As Horne reined up at the veranda, the sound of his arrival brought Cole to the door. There was no tone of welcome in Cole's voice. "Howdy, Charlie. Step down and come inside, wash the dust out of your throat."

Horne touched his hatbrim, then dismounted and walked up onto the veranda. Todd had risen. Facing him, Horne said, "I thought you might be here, Mr. Todd."

"Are you looking for me?" Todd asked.

"I'd like to have a word with you."

From within, Amos called, "Who is it?"

"Charlie Horne, Pa," Cole answered. He told Horne, "Come on inside."

"After you." Horne touched Todd's arm.

As they entered the parlor, Amos asked from his easy chair, "What brings you out here in all this heat, Charlie?"

"It's even hotter in town. Leg bothering you again, Amos?"

"It always acts up before a rain."

Horne pulled off his hat. He dug into a hip pocket and brought out a bright-red bandanna. Wiping it across his face, he said, "You reckon it's gonna rain?"

"Got to do it eventually," Amos answered.

Sarah and Asia came into the room. They exchanged greetings with Horne, then Sarah excused herself to the kitchen. Asia lingered in the doorway, her face questioning.

"Have a drink, Charlie," Amos gestured toward the bottles and glasses on the sideboard.

"I never drink while I'm on official business," Horne said.

Amos lifted a brow at him.

Cole was at the sideboard. As he poured himself a drink, he asked, "You've come out here on official business?"

Nodding, Horne flopped into a chair. He sprawled with his scuffed boots thrust out in front of him. For a moment, he looked thoughtfully at the toes. Then he looked up at Todd. "Mr. Todd, I'd be obliged if you'd tell me just exactly where you were when Don Edmund was killed."

"Just exactly when was Don Edmund killed?" Todd said.

"Sometime yesterday."

"I was here yesterday."

Amos spoke up in agreement. "Mr. Todd came out in the morning, and him and Asia and me rode up to the Indian spring together."

"But he left before dinner," Cole put in.

Horne glanced at Cole, then looked at Todd again. "About what time would you say you left here?"

Todd realized his hands were clenched, nails digging into

his palms. He forced them open. Forcing his voice to stay calm and level, he said, "I'm afraid I don't know. I failed to check my watch."

Asia interrupted. "Mister Horne, surely you don't think that Mr. Todd—"

"I ain't thinking anything yet, Missy," Horne answered. "I'm just trying to get the straight of who was where when Don Edmund got himself killed."

"Do you know when he was killed?" Amos asked. "Was it morning or afternoon?"

"Sometime after noon," Horne admitted. "We got a witness seen his horse in the bushes over near Samson's place around dinnertime. I reckon if we could find Samson's maid, Peggy Landers, she could tell us just when he left there. Only, she got out of town on the coach today."

"Do you think she could have killed him?" Asia asked.

Horne shook his head. "She could have put a bullet into him, but if she did, she wasn't alone in it. He was hauled from somewhere else and dumped under the bridge. It ain't possible a little tiny woman like Peggy Landers could have handled his weight all by herself."

"Why would she leave so suddenly if she didn't have something to do with the murder?"

"Samson fired her. He said he was sick of her sneaking around with Edmund all the time. He didn't want nothing happening with her like happened with Edith."

Cole winced. His hand, gripping the glass, whitened. He tossed down his drink, then turned tautly to pour himself another.

"Truth is, I don't think Peggy Landers had anything to do with the killing," Horne allowed.

Asia came forward to tower over him. "Well, Mr. Todd certainly couldn't have had anything to do with it!"

Horne looked up at her and said mildly, "He left here in the middle of the day. He didn't get back to town until real late. I checked with Bernie at the stable. He says he was there until twilight and Mr. Todd hadn't brought no horse in then, but it was in a stall when Bernie came back in the morning. Was a Pitchfork horse. Mr. Todd took it out again later."

Horne turned to Todd. "You mind telling me where you were between the time you left here and you got back to town?"

Todd minded. But he couldn't see any way out of it. Or any answer but the truth. "I rode up to have another look at the Indian spring. I spent most of the afternoon there."

"Anybody see you there?"

Todd looked at Cole. Cole glared at him. It was easy to see Cole would have preferred not to speak out. But there was a streak of honor in him he couldn't overcome.

"I seen him there," he admitted gruffly.

Horne pursed his lips, then asked, "You rode up to the spring with him?"

"No. I was here at the ranch when he left. I just figured he was going back to town. I hung around here awhile before I saddled up and went out to ride."

"You decided to follow him?" Horne asked.

Cole shook his head. "I wanted to think. I think best when I'm riding alone. I was just drifting around up in the badlands when I come across Todd's tracks. That was when I followed him and found him at the spring. But that wasn't until late on in the afternoon. I'd been riding a long while before that."

Horne looked at Todd. "That so? Were you up to the spring alone for a long while before Cole got there?"

Licking his lips, Todd nodded.

"And you didn't see anybody but Cole while you were up that way?"

"No."

Turning to Cole again, Horne asked, "You see anybody else while you were riding? You run across anybody who might of seen Mr. Todd up that way?"

Cole considered. He shook his head slowly. "I don't recall I seen anybody at all."

"Not the whole time you were riding?"

"No."

"*I* saw Mr. Todd," Asia said suddenly.

They all turned to look at her.

"Ma'am?" Horne said.

Her face was pale. She didn't meet his eyes as she told him, "*I* saw Mr. Todd. I rode after him—"

"You didn't," Cole snapped. "You were here when I left."

"I left just after you did," she answered. "But I followed Mr. Todd. I followed him directly to the spring. I was there with him all the time."

Cole's face reddened as he remembered finding Todd naked by the pool. He shouted at his sister, "Like hell!"

She met his glare defiantly. "I hid when you came. I knew how you'd feel if you found us together up there!"

"Sis!" he screeched at her.

Todd was on his feet now. He could feel the heat in his face and the tension in his shoulders. Asia was trying to help him, but she didn't know what she was implying. Or what Cole was thinking. He began, "Miss Asia, don't—"

She interrupted, facing him, almost shouting. "Don't call me a liar! I know you want to protect my good name, but don't call me a liar!"

Cole wheeled toward Todd and grabbed at his coat. "Todd, damn you! I'll kill you!"

"No, you won't," Horne told him. Rising, Horne rested a hand on the gun at his hip. His voice was cold, quiet, commanding. "You're not killing anybody else, Cole. I'm arresting you for the murder of Donald Edmund."

There was silence. A long, startled moment of it.

Amos exploded, "*What!*"

"Don't argue with me, Amos," Horne said. "I've already got it from his own mouth that he left here in the middle of the day and didn't see anybody as could witness for him until he got to Todd up at the spring. That gives him plenty of time to have done the killing. There ain't a body in Stick City don't know he had reason to do it. There's more than one man who heard him swear he'd kill Edmund."

"But . . ." Asia started. The word faded. She looked to Todd as if she thought he might be able to help.

But there was nothing Todd could do. Denying that Asia had been at the spring with him couldn't help Cole.

"Dammit!" Amos protested. "Charlie, you know damn well Cole never did it."

"I know he had a reason and he had the chance. It don't make a lick of difference what I feel personally. I got to arrest him."

"God damn," Cole grunted. He turned to his father in angry despair.

"He's wrong, boy, and I know it," Amos said. "Only, he's built a strong corral. It'll take me time to find the hole in it. I reckon, for now, you'd better go along with him."

Amos turned to Horne. "Let the boy say good-by to his Ma, will you? She's in the kitchen."

"Cole, you give me your word you won't run? You'll come peaceably with me?" Horne asked.

Cole hesitated. Slowly he said, "You got my word."

Horne moved away from him. Touching Todd's arm, he said, "Suppose you and me step outside awhile. Let these folks be alone."

Todd went onto the veranda with the deputy. As the door closed behind them, Todd asked, "Do you really believe Cole killed Edmund?"

"It don't matter what I believe. What matters is the evidence. Right now, the evidence points to him. Folks want somebody arrested. If I get me some better evidence that points somewhere else, I'll let Cole go and look somewhere else for the killer."

"If he were guilty, wouldn't you be taking a chance on leaving him inside that way? How do you know he won't go out the back way and escape?"

"I got his word."

"A man can lie."

Horne nodded. "Some men do. Might be Cole is lying about not killing Don Edmund. But he's given me his word he won't run now, and I believe that. Cole's a man who respects himself. How the hell could any man respect himself if his word wasn't no good?"

There was nothing Todd could say to that.

Amos appeared in the doorway. "Mr. Todd, I'm afraid Ma don't feel much like fixing up any fancy supper now. I reckon you'll understand."

"Of course," Todd said. "I'll be leaving now. About the money for the spa, if you'd like—"

"Please, not now, Mr. Todd," Amos said with a slow shake of his head. His voice was soft, a little hoarse, very distracted. "Right now, I got to see what I can do for my boy. I got to telegraph the high sheriff and a good lawyer over to Dadeston. I can't go messing around with anything else right now."

"But the railroad—"

"We've got along without a railroad up to now. I reckon we can manage. I'm sorry, Mr. Todd, but if you can't wait until I've got Cole clear, you'll just have to go on and forget about this spa here."

Todd had known it was coming. Even so, it hit him like a whiplash. For a moment, he couldn't catch his breath. He stood gazing at Amos, seeing the pale misery in the old man's face. And he knew it was all done.

Finally, he said, "Would you please say good-by to Miss Asia for me?"

It was a long ride back to town.

Todd rode slowly. Thoughtfully. He was trapped now. Caught between Groseille and Samson, with only Asia's sweet lie holding Deputy Horne at bay. Once Groseille's story came out, Asia would retract her lie. And that would be that.

If only his own damned lies had been truths . . .

He would have liked building a spa at the Indian spring. He would have liked watching Asia's face, seeing her joy and excitement as the dream turned to reality.

But lies were lies, and Groseille's trap was real, and there was no place to run—no way to outrun a telegraph message.

The sun was sinking, washing the basin with a ruddy glow, when he reached town. Leaving his horse at the livery stable, he walked toward the hotel. As he came up to the saloon, he caught the scent of whiskey. The appealing scent that promised a deep and dreamless sleep. He paused and looked over the batwings. There were people inside, talking and laughing. It was very tempting.

No, dammit, the answer wasn't in a bottle. If there was any answer at all, it was in his own cleverness. Only a sharp, sober search would find it.

In his room, he stripped and sprawled on the bed. The heat was heavy. Stifling. If only it would rain.

Well, rain or no rain, Millard Samson's plot against the McRaes had failed and the ranch was safe. And no matter what happened now, the McRaes would get their railroad. Samson knew that already.

Samson knew that.

Todd licked his lips as he considered. He had taken insurance of a sort against Samson before he left New York. If he could use it against Samson, perhaps he could use Samson against Groseille.

The idea was taking shape for him. He poked and prodded it, smoothing away its rough edges. Once it was fully formed, he slept.

CHAPTER 15

There was a morning breeze. It was spilling through the window, playing across Todd's body, when he woke. He rose, remembering the plans he had made before he slept. As he dressed, he went over the details. Maybe it would work. Maybe he would actually come out of this business with cash in his own pocket after all.

When he entered the barbershop, he met the same group of men who had been there the day before, discussing the murder. Today they were talking about Cole McRae, arguing his guilt. They seemed about equally divided.

The barber wanted to draw Todd into the conversation. He managed to flee after a few terse comments, hiding in the comfort of the tub. Eventually, he had to give that up. In the chair, being shaved, he had to listen to the barber. He didn't have to reply.

The breeze was skittering up the street as he left the barbershop. Looking north, into the wind, he could see a pale smear above the horizon. Clouds? Rain? A good sign? He couldn't tell at the distance.

He didn't believe in signs and omens.

After breakfast, he collected himself and headed for the *Sentinel* office.

The doors stood open, welcoming the breeze. Stepping inside, Todd breathed the scents of ink and paper. The first time he had gone there, before he met Andy Groseille, the odors had been pleasant. Now they seemed sinister, like a whiff of brimstone at one's deathbed.

The press groaned and clattered as Groseille twisted the devil's tail. The platen rose and he peeled a printed sheet off the form. He dropped it neatly onto a stack at his side, then looked up at Todd and nodded sociably.

"I've got to talk to you." Todd's voice was grim.

Groseille frowned. "Something wrong?"

"Everything," Todd answered. "The deal isn't going through."

Groseille hesitated, dark thoughts flickering in his face. "Then I suppose I should go ahead with the front page."

"Listen. There's nothing in it for you if you run that damned story."

"Oh, yes, there is!" Groseille made a broad gesture with one ink-stained hand. "I don't intend to spend the rest of my life setting type. *My* by-line is on that story as well as Don's. I'm keeping this paper going until his estate is settled. I'll do a damned good job of it. I'll show them I can edit and publish a paper. When I leave Stick City, it won't be to hunt another job as a compositor. If I can't go to Paris, I'll prove myself as an editor and get work in a real city. One where there are art studios. One where I can go on with my studies. I'll be a great artist someday. You're not stopping me, Mr. Fox!"

"I don't want to stop you. You have all my best wishes. There is no place I would rather you were than in Paris. I would be glad to help you in any way I could. But I *can't*. I haven't made a dollar in this town." Todd fished into a pocket and brought out a few coins. He held them toward Groseille on the palm of his hand. "That's *all* I have. Take half of it. Take more if you want it. Just leave me coach fare out of here."

Groseille snorted contemptuously at the coins. Very deliberately, he turned toward a bench where a form lay locked up. It was obviously the front page of the *Sentinel*. Among the columns of type there were blank blocks. Loosening a quoin, he slipped out the blanks. He pulled an engraving down from the shelf and put it into place. Todd could see that it was the picture of himself.

Unspeaking, Groseille went to the frame and picked up his

composing stick. His fingers danced over the case, dropping bits of type into the stick.

There was threat in every motion.

Todd watched for a long moment, then asked, "How much do you want?"

Groseille didn't look up. His fingers didn't hesitate. He said, "As much as I can get."

"Suppose I could raise a few hundred?"

"A few thousand would be more like it. Say ten thousand."

"Good God! What do you think I am?"

"A swindler, Mr. Fox. A very experienced swindler. But you won't swindle me. This story is worth a great deal to you. It might be worth your life. You'll pay for it. One way or another, you'll pay for it."

"I didn't kill Edmund. I would never be accused of that. Cole McRae has already been arrested. The matter is closed."

"No." Groseille shook his head. "He'll be cleared. Deputy Horne will need another suspect. All he needs to arrest you now is a motive. I've got the motive here in my hand."

"I couldn't have killed Edmund," Todd protested. "I have a witness to my whereabouts when he was killed."

"Do you? Do you really?" Groseille looked askance at Todd, obviously certain Todd had done the murder. "Do you have a witness who will swear in a court of law as to your presence when Don was murdered?"

"Yes," Todd lied.

"A reputable witness? One people will believe?"

"Yes."

Groseille sucked breath, his thoughts racing. "Well, suppose you never reached a court of law, Mr. Fox? What if you were tried by Judge Lynch? I can arrange it, you know. I'll have this paper on the streets tomorrow. People will believe what they read. I don't even have to lie about you. I can do it all with innuendo and implication. I can rouse a mob, incite a riot, make or break a man, all with this little stick." He waved the composing stick. "I have power in my hand, Mr. Fox! The power of life and death!"

Todd knew such things had been done. Often. He didn't know how good a propagandist Groseille might be, but that didn't matter. His own position was too precarious, too much founded on lies. It wouldn't require lynch law to put a noose around his neck. Asia had lied for him yesterday because she believed in him, but tomorrow once she knew the truth—

"I couldn't raise ten thousand if I robbed a bank," he said.

Groseille shrugged and his hand skimmed over the type case, dropping more words into the deadly little stick.

"I might manage two thousand," Todd suggested.

"Is your life something you'd bargain over as if it were a horse?"

"I can't do the impossible."

"Why don't you try robbing the bank?"

Todd wondered how much Samson would stand for. He said, "Suppose I could manage to raise five thousand?"

"I said *ten*."

"Five thousand is a lot of money. It would get you to Paris. A lot of students manage on a lot less. You must be as talented as they are, as dedicated as any of them."

Groseille smiled. "You have a slick tongue, Mr. Fox."

"How long would it take you to earn and save five thousand dollars working for a newspaper?" Todd asked.

Groseille's hand was still moving over the type case, but it slowed perceptibly.

"Five thousand," Todd said. "Or would you settle for less than Paris? What did you have in mind if you stay in the States, working for some newspaper in a city? Spend your days working at your job, and attend your art studies at night? In Paris, you'd study during the days. Your night would be your own. You know what Paris nights are."

Groseille's hand stopped. He turned slowly to face Todd. Gesturing toward the press, he said, "It will take me a couple of hours to finish what I'm running here. Then I have to put a story into that hole in the front page and run it off. I have a piece already set for that hole, eulogy to a great newspaperman, Donald Edmund."

He grinned suddenly as if he had made a joke. Then he went on, "If you're back here with five thousand dollars in cash before I lock up the form, that's the story I'll run. Otherwise, this one goes on press." He held out the stick.

"A couple of hours?" Todd said.

Groseille nodded.

The press was clattering again as Todd walked into the street.

The bank sat on a corner, with a large glass window facing onto each street. Both windows were painted over to above eye level. The double doors that angled across the corner were closed. Shoving one open, Todd stepped inside.

Millard Samson's bank had all the accouterments of prosperity. The walls were paneled chest high with polished mahogany. The brass Rochester lamps hanging from the ceiling were buffed to a golden sheen. The counter bisecting the room was of mahogany to match the walls, and the brass bars of the teller's cage were as shiny as the lamps.

The room was long and narrow. To one side, there were closed doors. Gold leaf on one read: MILLARD K. SAMSON, PRES.—PRIVATE. A scrawny, sandy-haired man who might have been thirty or forty or even fifty sat at a desk barring the way to Samson's door. He wore a stiff collar and a sour mouth. He was scribbling in a ledger as Todd approached him. He set his pen carefully into its holder and peered up at Todd through glasses that enlarged his eyes to almost twice their true size. The goggle eyes and his small, pouting mouth gave him an expression rather like a dead fish.

Considering Todd's apparel and manner, he reshaped the pout into something resembling a smile of welcome. "May I be of assistance, sir?"

Todd presented his card to the clerk. "I am here to see Mr. Samson."

The goggled eyes scanned the card. The clerk frowned. Uncertain, not wishing to offend, he asked, "Have you an appointment, sir?"

"Mr. Samson will see me," Todd said confidently.

"One moment, please, sir." Rising, the clerk brushed at his coat and tugged down its skirts. He adjusted the perch of his spectacles on his nose, then rapped cautiously at Samson's door.

From within, Samson snapped, "Yes?"

The clerk opened the door and stepped inside. He closed the door gently behind him.

Todd glanced around as he waited. He wondered what it would be like to rob a bank.

The clerk came out and told him, "Mr. Samson will see you, sir."

Samson's office was about what Todd had expected. The wall paneling gleamed. A lush carpet covered the floor. Heavy velour drapes with golden fringes masked the window. The desk Samson loomed behind was broad, neatly stacked with papers, ornamented with a whale-oil lamp of brass and crystal, and a matching inkstand. Samson's chair was high-backed, armed, upholstered with horsehide. A very comfortable swivel chair. The chair across the desk, provided for whoever faced Samson, was stiff and wooden. Like the one in Samson's den at home, it was not intended to put its occupant at ease.

A sideboard against one wall held a sparkling array of decanters and glasses. If he wished, Samson could counteract the effect of the stiff chair by offering a guest liquid hospitality.

There was no suggestion of hospitality in Samson's face or the set of his shoulders as he eyed Todd.

"Well?" he said.

Todd glanced at the decanters, then focused on Samson. "It's off."

"What?"

"McRae won't go for it. I had him on the hook when that deputy showed up and arrested his son."

"And you let that stop you?"

"I can only do so much. I couldn't pull a gun on him and

force him into it. Right now he isn't interested in anything but getting his son out of jail."

"Hell," Samson muttered. His gaze narrowed. "Fox, I've sunk a lot of money into this. I want that mortgage."

"You won't get it. Not through me."

"You'll do what I tell you."

Todd shook his head. "I'm leaving on the coach out tomorrow."

"The hell you are!" Samson snapped. "I've bought and paid for you. I'll tell you what you do and don't do."

Stepping to the sideboard, Todd chose a decanter, opened it, and sniffed. A very good cognac. With a small nod of approval, he helped himself to a glass. He sampled the cognac, then said, "You bought yourself the wrong man. You told me no one here would know about James Fox."

"Someone does?" Samson asked warily.

"Groseille, at the *Sentinel*. He has the whole story of that business in France written already. Now he's planning to print it."

"Stop him."

Todd looked at Samson, wondering if he meant commit a murder. "I can't."

"Why not?"

"He's run off copies already, and put them away somewhere. If anything happens to him, they get mailed to newspapers and the sheriff."

"Then you're finished."

"Not yet. Groseille will listen to reason. If it's spelled out in gold."

Samson snorted, "You're in trouble and you think I'll buy you out of it?"

"*You're* in trouble," Todd told him. "I think you'll buy yourself out of it. I'm the middleman who'll keep your hands clean when you do it."

"I'm in trouble?" Samson didn't believe it. He scowled at Todd, defying him to offer an explanation.

Todd gestured with the brandy glass. "If I go down, I take

you with me. This was your swindle. You'll pay for it—one way or another."

"You'll talk?" Samson asked. He seemed unperturbed by the threat.

Todd nodded.

Samson leaned back in his chair. He folded his hands over his gut and eyed Todd. "What makes you think anyone would believe you? You're a damned convicted swindler, Fox. You haven't spoken an honest word since you arrived in this town. Once the townspeople know who you really are, they'll know you've lied to them. Why should they listen to you? Hell, I'll tell them you came here and tried to blackmail me with this wild scheme, this threat of false accusations. I'm an innocent victim, the same as the rest."

He swung to his feet and started around the desk. "I'll tell them now!"

"No." Todd's voice was level. There was no sign of tension in his face. But the hand that held the glass was pale, almost white. "No, you're mistaken. I'm afraid I'm the one they'll believe. You see, I have proof that you're implicated up to your ass."

"The hell! The goddamned hell I am! I never put a thing in writing. There aren't any witnesses. I made sure there was no way they could connect us. There's nothing! Nothing, Fox, but your word against mine."

"There are details. You know the expense money you gave me in New York? I put a good part of it into research. I found out you had seen railroad officials. You knew there was a spur line planned to Dadeston. You paid off to have that news kept quiet. I can tell a lot of little details, Samson. Anyone who wants to bother can check the same way I did, and find out what I learned. If I talk, someone will bother. Someone like Andy Groseille. If my own background is checked, it will be obvious that *somebody* financed me. Somebody bought me these clothes and paid my fare here. Once I've told the people where to look, they'll find the truth. The *whole* truth."

Samson turned away from Todd. He went to the sideboard and poured himself a drink. He downed it, refilled the glass, then turned to Todd again. The fire in his eyes was hot enough to burn, to kill.

Finally he said, "How much do you want?"

How much would he go for? Todd wondered. He said, "Ten thousand."

"You bastard," Samson muttered softly.

"Ten thousand isn't a lot to pay for all this." Todd indicated the opulent office, and all that it implied.

Samson's gaze followed the gesture as he considered Todd's meaning.

"You have a nice home," Todd added. "A lovely wife."

Samson gave an abstract nod. His thoughts weren't on his home. He breathed deeply, sighed, and said, "I'll have the money for you later."

"I'd like it now."

"I can't give it to you now. I'll have to—uh—make some entries in the books. After the bank closes. Come back tonight. After dark."

That would mean stalling Groseille longer. But Todd knew Samson couldn't be pushed any faster. He asked, "Here, or your house?"

"Here. I'll be working late. Knock at the window. I'll come to the door and let you in. Come after dark."

"You'd rather no one saw me?"

Samson nodded.

Todd finished the cognac. As he started for the door, Samson asked him, "Did Don Edmund know about Fox?"

"Yes. He and Groseille wrote the story together."

"You're lucky he's dead," Samson said. "I don't think you could have bought him off."

Yes, Todd thought. He said nothing. As he walked out of the office, the clerk gave him another sour little smile. He didn't bother to return it.

CHAPTER 16

Groseille was working at the press when Todd walked into the *Sentinel* office. He pulled a printed sheet, then turned to Todd. There were smudges of ink on his face, and his eyes were weary. His expression at the sight of Todd mixed hope and doubt. "That was quick."

"I don't have it yet," Todd said.

The hope in Groseille's face faded. Suspiciously he asked, "You expect to get it?"

"Tonight. I'll bring it to you in the morning before I take the coach out."

"No!"

"What do you mean, *no?* You want the damned money, don't you?"

"Morning's too late. I've almost finished this run." Groseille patted the press. "When it's done, I'll be ready to lock up the front page and put it on press. I plan to run it tonight."

"Go ahead and print it with Edmund's eulogy. I'll have the money for you."

"I want the money in my hand *before* I start printing. I won't know which story to print until I *see* the money."

"Dammit, I've got to have time to get it."

"I've got to have time to print the paper. I'll have to run the front page tonight. I intend to have copies collated and on the street before Don's funeral tomorrow." Groseille smiled suddenly. "Ed White, the editor of the Dadeston *Gazette*, is coming in for the funeral. That's why we put it off until tomorrow. I'm going to have this paper on the street when he gets here. I'm going to give him a copy. Put it into his hands myself. If I have a first-class story to break, it's going to be in that paper."

"I can't get the money until tonight. Sometime after sunset. Either you hold off printing that story and you get your five thousand in cash as soon as I have it, or else you go on with your damned paper and print your damned story and impress your damned Ed White, and lose your chance to go back to Paris," Todd said.

Groseille rubbed an inky hand at his face. When he drew it away, there was another dark smear across his forehead.

Todd added, "When I bring you the money, I want to see a proof of the front page *without* that story in it."

"No," Groseille muttered. But he wasn't refusing, just objecting to the situation. He studied his thoughts.

"Paris," Todd said.

Groseille nodded. Slowly he said, "You bring me the money tonight, before midnight. If you aren't here by midnight, I'll set the story and run it. I won't have the whole run complete by morning, but I'll have enough copies to spread them around. I'll have a copy to show you before your coach leaves. I'll have copies with that story on the coach. You understand me, Fox?"

"I'll bring you the money as soon as I get it. Will you be here?"

"Yeah. Without Don to help, I'm 'way behind. I should have had the whole damned thing printed by now. If I sleep at all, it'll be a quick nap here." Groseille nodded toward a rumpled cot in a back corner.

"It's a hard business, being a newspaperman?" Todd said.

"Yes." Suddenly Groseille grinned. Very confidently he said, "But I won't be one for much longer."

As Todd walked out, the press clattered behind him. The sound was mocking, ominous, like some huge crushing machine stalking him. He hurried away from it.

The saloon was a temptation. Determined, he strode past it and into the hotel. There was no one behind the desk. The lobby had a musty, dead smell to it. The stairs were dimly lit.

He climbed to the gloom of the second floor and shoved open the door to his room.

A man stood facing him.

Startled, he frowned at the figure silhouetted against the open window. It took him a moment to make out the shadowed features.

"Cole McRae?"

"Come in and shut that door." Cole's voice was jagged with anger.

"I thought you were in jail," Todd said.

"I was, but I ain't now. Get in here." Back-stepping to keep distance between Todd and himself, Cole motioned Todd into the room. The hand he gestured with held a gun. He leveled it at Todd's gut. This time it was cocked.

This time, Todd thought, Cole was prepared to kill. And again, Todd felt the urge to keep living that was stronger than any argument made of words. No matter what his life was, he wanted to keep it. He licked his lips. It wasn't easy keeping his voice even. "What do you want?"

"Take off your coat."

"Why?" Todd asked as he slipped out of the coat and dropped it on the bed.

"I want to beat hell out of you," Cole told him. "I ain't got a horsewhip handy. I'll have to do it with my fists."

Todd understood. He said, "Your sister was lying. She was never with me at the Indian spring."

"Asia don't lie. Now take off that vest."

"She was lying this time." Todd fingered open the vest buttons. He tossed the vest on top of the coat. His shirt was soaked with sweat, plastered to his body. Sweat dampened his hair and trickled along his brows. He would have liked to take the shirt off too. He asked himself what the hell it mattered now if Cole saw the scars on his back. But he realized he was ashamed of the scars. And ashamed that Asia had lied for him.

"The pistol," Cole was saying. "Pull it out real easy and put it on the bed."

Todd tugged the little Remington from his waistband. As he set it on the bed, he wondered why he had bothered carrying it. Straightening, he faced Cole. His mouth was dry now, and his heart pounding. His hands closed themselves into fists at his sides.

Cole eased down the hammer of the revolver. He flung the gun onto the bed and lunged.

One fist was flying toward Todd's face. The other aimed at his gut.

Todd pivoted, throwing up an arm to fend the blow to his face. His body twisted and the fist meant for his gut caught him in the side. It was a hard, slamming blow and it jolted him.

His own left jabbed at Cole's breastbone. One good connection there would spasm Cole's lungs, setting him back gasping for wind. But Todd's knuckles hit rib bone plated with muscle that felt like sheet iron.

Cole grunted. And the fist that had hit Todd's side drove a hammer blow at the back, for the kidney.

Todd flinched at the pain that knifed through him. This wasn't going to be by the Marquis of Queensberry rules. No gentlemen's sparring. Cole was attacking to inflict punishment, no matter how. He tried again for the kidney.

Awkwardly, Todd slammed a hand at Cole's arm. It deflected the blow just enough. Cole's fist hit the bone of Todd's hip.

For an instant Todd's leg was pained. Numbed.

Cole jerked back his hand, giving it a shake, as if he had hurt himself. Then he was charging again. His left was high, and his right low. The left was a feint. The right meant business.

Flinging up his own right, Todd struck aside Cole's left. At the same time, Todd countered with his left, slashing at Cole's right wrist with the outer edge of the stiff, open hand. It didn't stop Cole's right hook, but it took the steam out of it.

No rules, Todd thought. And he kicked. His boot hit Cole in the shin.

Cole staggered back from him, and he saw the flash of pained surprise in Cole's face.

Todd lunged, a fist aimed for Cole's face, another for the breastbone.

Throwing up both hands, Cole caught and blocked them both. Todd threw a knee up at Cole's groin.

It was a glancing blow. It startled Cole more than it hurt him. Apparently there was a rule in his book against that. His mouth moved, shaping curses that he didn't find voice for, and the burning anger in his eyes flared.

Ducking his head, he plowed at Todd's body with fists pistoning.

Todd aimed at Cole's face again. His knuckles rammed along Cole's cheek as Cole caught him in the gut. He gasped breath, half doubling. With one hand, he grabbed at the fist that Cole was driving toward the same spot. The other, which had hit Cole's cheek, opened. Its edge slashed at Cole's neck.

Wincing, Cole jerked up his head. Todd's fingers were wrapped around his wrist. He jerked against the thumb, pulling free, flinging the fist toward Todd's gut again.

Todd's fist tried for Cole's breastbone. Hit. And Cole staggered back, gasping.

Todd's gut ached. He hesitated, sucking breath himself.

Cole glared at him. There was a thin streak of blood on Cole's cheek where Todd's ring had cut a shallow gash.

First blood, Todd thought, and knew it was meaningless. No referee was counting points here.

Suddenly, with a shouted *en garde*, Todd lunged. He feinted toward Cole's gut. He felt the shoulder seam of his shirtsleeve rip as he drove an uppercut toward Cole's chin.

Cole jerked back his head an instant before Todd's knuckles connected. One hand was swinging toward Todd's arm, trying to shove aside the blow. The other fist was going for Todd's chest. Todd's fist caught the edge of Cole's jaw and skidded up to his ear. Cole's fist connected with Todd's chest.

Todd staggered back.

Growling deep in his throat, Cole swung for Todd's face. Todd tried to duck. Tried to block. The block missed. The duck wasn't quick enough. Cole's fist smashed into one corner of Todd's mouth, crushing his lip against his teeth. Todd felt the surge of pain and the sudden taste of salt.

Cole caught him in the chest again.

And again.

Todd's lungs cramped and there was blood in his throat. He felt as if he were choking. He had to catch breath. Crouching, his arms hugged to his chest, he back-stepped.

Cole paused, giving him an instant of rest.

Todd ended the instant suddenly. Lunging, he grabbed at Cole. Pulled Cole toward him. Spun on one foot. Caught Cole with a hard fist in the side. He flung himself against Cole. Rammed a knee at Cole's groin again. Missed.

He was off balance, clutching at Cole. And then they were both falling. Cole sprawled on his back, with Todd on top of him. Even as he hit the floor, Cole was squirming to escape. But Todd didn't mean to pin him. Not right now. Coughing and rolling, Todd came up on his knees a long stride away from Cole.

He spat blood and sucked breath. His mouth felt thick and numb.

Cole scrambled onto his knees and stopped there. Now he needed a moment's breath, a moment's rest, too. He rubbed the back of a hand against his jaw and scowled at Todd.

"There's more to you than I figured," he allowed, his voice hoarse.

Todd worked his mouth. Spat more blood.

Cole asked him, "I bust your ribs?"

He shook his head. His lips worked awkwardly. His words came thick and misshapen. "I never touched your sister."

It was the wrong thing to say. Cole jerked himself to his feet and attacked.

Todd was still on his knees. He got a foot on the floor, coming up as Cole dived for him.

Ducking his chin, he rose. He shoved with the foot against the floor, driving his head at Cole's face. He hit. Hard. The shock of it jolted him, shuddering down his spine, and he dropped to his knees again.

Cole staggered back, hands pressed to his face. Blood trickled between his fingers. He kept staggering until his back was against the wall.

On his feet now, Todd stood crouching, hands fisted. Ready, but unmoving. Grabbing this moment more of rest.

Cole's shoulders pressed against the wall. He pulled his hands away from his face. Blood spewed from his nose. It looked broken. He gasped breath through his mouth, his chest heaving. He frowned at his bloody hands.

Then at Todd.

Todd searched for the words that might put an end to this damn-fool fight.

Cole shook his head slowly, like a wounded bear. He had the look about him of a pit bear, cornered and hurt, with the dogs yapping around him, playing him a moment before they pressed their attack to the finish.

Todd had watched bearbaiting often enough, but he had never found any pleasure in it. It always seemed so pointless. Fine, strong animals pitted against each other, fighting, suffering, dying, just for the amusement of jaded tastes.

He realized there weren't any words that would stop Cole. Like a pit bear, Cole would go on fighting until one of them was unconscious. Or dead.

Cole was leaning against the wall. With a grunt, he straightened. He took his weight on the balls of his feet.

As Cole lunged, Todd snatched up the revolver from the bed. It was a big gun. Heavy. He hefted it upward. Cole was slamming toward him. He stood braced for the force of the attack.

Cole saw the gun upraised in Todd's hand. But it was too late. He couldn't stop himself. He couldn't duck. He rammed into Todd. And Todd smashed the gun down into the side of Cole's head.

Todd was off balance. Cole was falling, dragging Todd down. Then they were both on the floor, with Cole on top, his weight heavy, crushing on Todd.

It was limp weight. Motionless. Cole's head lay on Todd's shoulder. The shallow, broken snatching of breath was a loud grating in Todd's ear. Still clutching the gun, Todd shoved at Cole's body and wriggled from under it.

The surge of strength, the power of tension, that had carried Todd through the fight, suddenly left him. His knees trembled and his hands shook. He felt sick. Dizzy. Sidestepping, he slumped to sit on the bed.

His arms rested on his knees, the heavy gun dangling loosely in his hand. He sat head-hung, his own breathing erratic and the pounding of his heart a sharp thunder in his chest. Blood trickled from the corners of his mouth. A drop fell on his sleeve.

Squinting to focus, he saw that the sleeve was spattered with blood. Some was his own. He supposed some was Cole's. He looked down at Cole.

Cole lay on his side on the floor. His eyes were closed. His mouth gaped open slackly. His nose was skewed and still bleeding. His whole face was smeared red.

Too damned much blood, Todd thought wearily. His hands were stained with it. Suddenly he wanted very badly to have them clean.

His body ached as he got himself onto his feet. He had to force his legs to carry him to the commode. There was water in the pitcher. He set down the gun and tried to tilt the pitcher over the basin. He could hardly lift the damned thing. Finally he got a couple of inches of water into the basin and set the pitcher aside.

When he dipped his hands into the water, it took on a tinge of pink. He rinsed them thoroughly, then dumped the dirty water into the slop jar. There was more in the pitcher.

This time it was easier to tilt the pitcher. This time when

he dipped his hands into the basin, the water didn't change color. He caught both hands full and splashed it into his face. Even tepid, it felt soothingly cool against the heat of his flesh.

Water was a very fine thing, he thought. All kinds of water. Bath water. Rain water. Drinking water. Spring water. Dammit, he wished it would rain. He wished he were at the Indian spring, soaking in the mineral water. He wished he could see Asia just once more. It would have been good to go to the spring with her. Good to be as guilty as Cole McRae thought him to be.

Damn!

He rinsed his hands again, wet a corner of the towel, and scrubbed his face. His mouth was swelling and there were sore spots that would probably be the ugly yellow-blue of bruises before long. He would look like hell tomorrow. But it wouldn't matter. Tomorrow, he would be gone.

He felt stronger now. Strong enough to manage the pitcher. He took a mouthful of water from it, then spat. He did it again, and again, until he couldn't taste blood any longer. Then he took a deep drink of water.

Behind him, Cole groaned.

Snatching up the gun, Todd wheeled.

Cole's head moved slightly. Still groaning, he blinked open his eyes. The groaning stopped. His bloody face wrinkled into a frown. Stiffly, he twisted himself. He got a hand on the floor and braced. With effort, he sat up. Leaning on one hand, he touched the other gently to his face. He explored his nose with his fingertips. For a very long moment, he seemed puzzled.

The bewilderment faded. His eyes narrowed as he looked at Todd.

The gun filled Todd's hand. The hammer was high but not awkward. Todd's thumb rested on it, ready to pull it back, if necessary.

Cole eyed the gun.

"Don't get up," Todd said.

Cole looked as if he had meant to try. He didn't look as if he could have made it.

Hoarse-voiced, his mouth swollen and his words slurred, Todd said, "Listen to me, goddammit. Don't move. Just listen. *I never touched your sister*. Can't you understand that? I never *tried* to touch her."

With his nose broken, Cole's voice was a muffled growl. He spoke slowly, catching breath between words. "She said she was with you. You were damned jaybird naked and she was there."

"She lied."

"She don't lie."

"She did this time. Why the hell is it so much easier for you to believe your sister would play the whore to me than it is for you to believe she'd tell a small, innocent lie for me?"

Cole frowned.

"Think, man!" Todd insisted. "She was certain I hadn't killed Edmund. But it looked like Deputy Horne thought I had. She was only trying to save me trouble. That's *all!*"

"She don't lie," Cole repeated. This time his tone wasn't so positive.

"She *did* lie. She would have told the same lie for you if Horne had asked your whereabouts first. Can't you understand that?"

Cole shook his head as if he couldn't understand. He said again, "She don't lie." But the words were only an echo of his confusion. He rubbed his hand at his face and gave another shake of his head, trying to clear his thoughts. He was dazed, puzzled, but the certainty that had driven him to fight was gone now.

Sighing, Todd slumped into the chair. The hand holding the gun rested in his lap. He felt too weary to go on arguing.

Finally Cole looked up at him and said, "She lied?"

"Yes!"

Cole took a deep, rasping breath. Slowly, softly, to himself, he said, "She lied."

He looked at the gun resting in Todd's lap. Keeping his

eyes on it, he hoisted himself cautiously from the floor. He stood with his feet spread, tottering, waiting for Todd to react.

Todd said nothing.

Cole stumbled to the commode, found the basin, and dipped water from it. He wiped a wet hand at his bloody face and winced.

"I think my nose is busted," he mumbled.

Todd asked, "You want a doctor?"

Running his hand up the side of his head, Cole found a painful knot where Todd had buffaloed him with the big revolver. He added, "I think my skull is cracked."

That was a real possibility. The idea frightened Todd. He didn't want to have seriously injured Asia's brother. Pulling himself up out of the chair, he made a reaching gesture toward Cole. "Come on. I'd better get you to a doctor."

CHAPTER 17

The doctor's name was Durfee. His infirmary was in his home, a neat, white house behind a neat, white picket fence, just off the main street. It wasn't far from the hotel.

He was a young man, and he seemed appalled at the sight of Cole's battered face. Todd guessed this was his first practice and he was still new at his job. He hoped the doctor knew his business.

Dr. Durfee restrained the curiosity that showed in his face. He kept his manner grave and formal, as befit a man of his position. Leaving Todd in the parlor, he escorted Cole into a back room.

It took a while, but when Cole emerged his steps were steady and the glassy, vacant look was gone from his eyes. He peered at Todd over a mass of bandage plastered to his face.

"Now you, sir," The doctor gestured for Todd to come into the back room.

Cole started for the door.

Rising, Todd stepped in front of him. "One thing?"

Cole grunted in question.

"How did you get out of jail?"

"Turned out a couple of fellers from the Long J seen me out riding." Cole's voice was nasal, blurred and stiff. "They told Charlie Horne. Worked out I couldn't of killed Edmund and got up to the spring by the time I did—"

He stopped suddenly, his eyes narrowing. He scowled at Todd with dark suspicion. "Now you're gonna go tell Charlie that I wasn't up to the spring when I said I was after all?"

"That would be a lie, wouldn't it?" Todd said.

Cole nodded warily.

Todd shrugged.

"Now you, sir," the doctor said again.

Todd turned to follow him.

"Todd," Cole said.

Looking back over his shoulder, Todd asked, "What?"

Reluctantly, as if it hurt a lot to do it, Cole said, "Maybe I was wrong about you."

"You were," Todd said.

Cole stalked to the door and slammed out of the room.

The doctor eyed Todd in fascinated speculation. Todd said nothing. Slumping with disappointment, the doctor led him into the back room.

It was a well-equipped office, complete with an articulated skeleton in one corner. The skull grinned at Todd. Another time, he might have grinned back.

He seated himself in the chair the doctor indicated. As the doctor set out his mysterious bottles and swabs, Todd asked, "Will he be all right?"

"The nose will mend."

"I mean his head."

"He'll have quite a lump and a headache, but that's the worst of it," Durfee said. "What did you hit him with?"

Todd couldn't recall admitting that he was the one who had done the damage. Durfee was prying, guessing. But it was no secret. At least it wouldn't be one for long in this town. He answered, "A revolver."

Durfee dipped a swab and touched it to a cut on Todd's cheek. Todd flinched at the sting. "Hold still. Open your mouth."

Todd obeyed.

"You must have been really mad at him," Durfee commented, peering at the cut inside Todd's lip. "I'd recommend washing that with whiskey. You can close it now."

Todd closed his mouth and tested the cut with his tongue, then said, "I wasn't mad at him at all."

Durfee gave a shake of his head. "I'll never understand you

Westerners. You're uncivilized. Totally uncivilized. All of you."

Todd did grin then. It was a small, somewhat pained grin.

He paid Durfee, but offered no explanations. He left the doctor standing in the doorway looking thoroughly puzzled.

Wash it with whiskey, he thought, and he considered buying a bottle. He could take it to his room. Wash the cut thoroughly while he waited for nightfall.

But that was no good. There was nothing but trouble in a whiskey bottle.

Turning onto the main street, he headed for the hotel.

His shirt was spattered with blood. He had tucked in the tails and buttoned his coat over the stains before he left the hotel with Cole. But there was no way of covering his face. People he passed glanced at him covertly, or stared outright. Some had been there, staring, when he helped Cole down the street and asked directions to the doctor's office. He supposed the gossip and speculations were already spreading. He wondered what people thought and what they would be saying. He hoped Asia's name wouldn't come into it.

That was the real pain. The fear of hurting her.

He saw her suddenly. She was coming toward him, hurrying at him with her eyes fixed on him. She looked frightened.

He didn't want to face her. But he could hardly run away. Not when she was just a few steps from him. He licked his lips, swallowed, and met her.

"Mr. Todd! You're hurt! What happened?" She was looking at his mouth. And then at the bit of shirt showing between the lapels of his coat. He thought there must be blood showing on the shirt.

"Miss Asia," he said, with a small bow of formal greeting. He touched his fingertips to his swollen mouth and forced a smile. "Nothing serious."

"That's blood." She frowned at his shirt front. Then she looked into his eyes. "Cole?"

She had made a good guess. There was no way Todd could deny it. Cole would be going home with his face battered and his nose broken. Even if Todd lied now, she would learn the truth then.

He nodded.

"Oh, no!" she said. "I knew he was—I—I didn't think he was—are you hurt?"

"No," he insisted. He wanted to change the subject. "You know Cole was released? Deputy Horne found witnesses who cleared him."

"Uh huh. Pa and I came in to telegraph Dadeston and we went by the jail and Cole was already gone." Suddenly there was joy in her face. "You know what this means! Everything is all right now! We can go on with the spa. Pa is on his way to the bank now to negotiate the mortgage with Mr. Samson and—"

"No!"

"What?"

"No!" Todd said. "You've got to stop him!"

"I don't understand—"

"Miss Asia, it's all over. Forget it. Don't let your father mortgage the ranch to Samson."

"But why? Mr. Todd, please, it isn't too late! We can get the money for you today." She stopped, her confusion suddenly slashed by an ugly thought. "Is it because of Cole? You won't deal with us now because of him?"

"No, not that." Even as he said it, Todd knew he was making a mistake. He could have accepted the excuse and escaped, leaving her to think him simply vindictive.

"Then what?" she asked. "Please, we *need* the railroad."

"You'll have your railroad. It's already planning to build into Dadeston. That's close enough for you, isn't it? It will come here, spa or no spa. You'll be able to ship your cattle. Believe me, you've got to stop your father. No matter what you do, don't let Samson get his claws into Pitchfork. He'll steal it from under you."

"But all the things you told us—"

"Lies. All lies." As he said it, he pushed past her. He strode rapidly down the walk, wanting to escape her.

She hurried after him.

As she came up to his side, she grabbed his arm. He jerked away from her touch. "Stop your father! If you want to save Pitchfork, stop him now! Quickly!"

The saloon was just ahead. He almost ran the last few steps away from her. He slammed through the batwings. They squealed harshly behind him.

Stepping to the bar, he darted a sideways glance at the doorway. Asia stood outside. She couldn't enter. It wasn't proper. No decent woman would walk into a saloon like this.

But Asia didn't always do what was proper.

Todd could see her uncertainty. She was tempted to follow him in. Why the hell couldn't she go away? Why couldn't she do what he had told her?

The bartender came over to Todd and made some comment. Unheeding, Todd asked for whiskey. The bartender put a glass in front of him and filled it. He emptied it. The whiskey burned the cut in his mouth. Grimacing, he put down the glass and asked for another. From the corner of his eyes, he could see Asia still standing there.

Go, dammit! he thought. *Stop him now. Don't make me do it!*

He downed the second drink and called for a third. Time was passing. If Amos was to be stopped, someone would have to move. If Asia wouldn't do it, then Todd knew he must. But if he did, he would be destroying his only chance of escape. He would be putting his own neck in a noose.

At last Asia turned and walked away.

Todd tasted the drink, waiting a moment. Then he went to the door. Over the batwings, he could see Asia heading toward the bank. She walked slowly at first, deep in her own thoughts. As she understood what Todd had said, she increased her pace. Finally she reached the bank and disappeared into it.

Todd felt a moment of deep relief.

But he knew she would be back. Amos would be with her. No social customs could prevent Amos from walking into a saloon. Amos would demand an explanation. But the only explanation Todd had was the truth. He didn't want Asia to know the truth. Let her think anything else she chose to think about him. But not the truth.

He swallowed down the drink, paid, and left.

Back in his hotel room, he bolted the door behind him.

There was one more clean shirt in his traveling case. He took it out and spread it on the bed, then stripped the bloody shirt and stuffed it into the case. He put both cases by the window. They were nice cases. Expensive. Worth money in any pawn shop.

He put on the fresh shirt, tucked in the tails, and stuck the little Remington into the waistband of his trousers. The gun would be worth money in a pawn shop too. He buttoned the vest over it, then tugged on his coat. With luck, he wouldn't need a pawn shop. He would have five thousand dollars of Millard Samson's money in his pocket when he left.

He hoped.

He glanced around the room and took a last look at himself in the mirror. The swollen mouth distorted his image. The eyes looked odd to him. The image in the glass seemed a stranger. Not Fox. Not Todd. Who?

Without an answer, he turned away from the mirror. He lowered the traveling cases through the window to the shed roof below, then followed them. On the roof, he looked at the sky.

It was still uncertain, still hinting rain without making promises. And the sun was still well above the far horizon. There was a lot of time to be killed before dark.

He dropped the cases to the ground, then slipped over the edge of the roof and let himself down. He stowed the cases in the corner where the shed met the building. For a moment, he stood looking at them, wondering if he would be back to collect them. So many things were going wrong. So much more could go wrong before the coach left the next day.

Maybe he ought to leave now. Hire a horse and head out. Run like hell before the trap snapped closed and there was no escape. He still had a few dollars in his pocket, and the gold ring on his finger. He could get a long way from Stick City on that. Maybe all the way to San Francisco. Surely they had slums where a man could drink himself to death in San Francisco.

But if he ran now, Groseille would print that story. Asia would learn the truth about James Todd Fox. And Millard Samson wouldn't be out ten thousand dollars.

That thought irked Todd. It had been Samson's swindle. Samson was as much a damned thief as he was. Samson should pay something, somehow.

With his decision made, Todd walked toward the end of the alley. His problem for the time being was simply to stay out of sight until after dark.

Across the alley, behind the hardware and furniture store, there was a barn. The doors stood open. As he came up to them, Todd glanced inside.

The barn was a carriage house. It held a cart, a dray, and a hearse. A man in dirty work clothes was dabbing at the hearse with a wet paintbrush. He looked up at Todd and smiled. "Howdy."

"Good afternoon," Todd answered, taking a step into the barn. Despite its open doors, the big shed was gloomy, its shadows deep and thick. It had the feeling of a hole. A hiding place.

"Looking for somebody, mister?" the man with the paintbrush asked.

Todd shook his head. Conversationally, he said, "Are you getting ready for a funeral?"

"Yep." The workman brushed a patch of black over a scratch on the hearse. "Gonna bury Don Edmund in the morning. Should of buried him yesterday, but there's some bigwig from Dadeston coming to see them shovel him in."

This was as good a place, as good a way, to kill time as any. Todd said, "I suppose it will be a big affair."

The painter grinned. "I don't know. Edmund didn't have a

lot of what you'd call *friends* around here. Not men friends, leastways."

"Women friends?"

"Mostly married ones." The painter's grin was sly and insinuating. "He thought he was hell on wheels with the women."

"Wasn't he?"

"I reckon he was. Ain't likely they'll come out in public wearing black for him, though. Now, for a real funeral, you should have seen when Wilt Miller's missus died. Sweet woman, that. Folks come from all over the county to see her funeral. It was last spring and there had been some rain and there was flowers aplenty. Real pretty funeral. I reckon she went to heaven a happy woman."

"You like funerals."

"Sure! Don't everybody?"

"I've never cared much for them myself."

"Likely you never been to a real proper one, then."

"Perhaps."

"Now, we put on a good funeral here in Stick City. See this here buggy?" The painter waved his brush at the hearse. "You might not expect to see such a fine one out here in a little place like Stick City. But folks around here don't skimp none on funerals. Every funeral we have, I touch her up, get her spick and span for it. We're right proud of our funerals here."

Todd looked critically at the hearse. It had obviously seen better days. The hard-rubber tires were cracked. The flaking paint had been retouched until it was piled up like scabs. The gilt was faded and scuffed. Even in the dimness, he could see moth holes in the drapery.

"Fine, ain't she?" the painter said.

Todd nodded. "Yours?"

"Well, you might say she really belongs to Mr. Hamp, owns the furniture store. But I'm the one keeps her and drives her. Nobody but me. I got me a black coat and a silk hat with a black fancy in the band. I cut a fine figure on that seat."

He gestured at the seat. It was only a plank bench, a crude, bare, backless, sideless board held up by a pair of unadorned supports. It looked out of place. A wart on the ornate hearse.

Glancing at Todd, the painter realized his hearse wasn't showing at its best. He reached under the seat and pulled out a folded cloth.

"Hammercloth," he told Todd. "Help me put it on?"

Todd gave him a hand, shaking dust out of the black velvet and straightening its tarnished gold fringes. Then they spread it over the bench, and the painter adjusted its drape until the entire seat was covered.

Todd nodded approval.

Grinning, the painter reached under the hammercloth and produced a small, brown bottle, He uncorked it, took a gulp from it, then wiped the neck with his hand and held it toward Todd.

According to the label, it was a cough syrup suitable for men, women, children, and animals. Todd sampled it cautiously. At least two-thirds pure alcohol, he thought, with a dash of opium and wild-cherry flavoring. He took only a small sip, then returned the bottle. The painter hid it again under the seat of the hearse. A fitting place for it, Todd thought.

He lingered, watching the painter work on the hearse, listening to him meander about funerals, waiting in this safe hole as the daylight faded.

The painter finished up by lantern light. When he was done, he invited Todd to continue the conversation at the saloon. Politely, Todd declined. The twilight was almost gone. In moments, it would be full dark. He took his leave of the painter and headed for the bank.

CHAPTER 18

Todd turned from the alley into a side street. At the intersection with the main street, he stopped. The lanterns in front of the saloons were lit, and there were people on the walks. He looked up the street and down it. To his relief, he saw no sign of Asia or Amos McRae. Collecting himself, he rounded the corner and headed for the bank.

He had to pass the *Sentinel* office. He expected it to be open, with Groseille busy at the press. But the doors were shut, the office silent and dark. Surprised, he tried a door. It opened. He stepped inside.

"Groseille?" he called softly.

There was no answer.

But Groseille was supposed to be there, waiting for him to bring the money. He felt a sick, hollow fear that something had gone wrong.

Fingering in a pocket, he found his matchbox. The scent of sulphur puffed into his face as he struck a match. The smell of hell and brimstone.

Holding up the match, he glanced around the office. The big press loomed behind the counter. There was a form on its bed. Perhaps the front page. He started to walk back and look at it. Then he saw the man lying face down on the cot in the far corner. He could barely make out the sprawled shape in the shadows. Groseille taking a nap, he thought. There was no point in waking the printer. It might lead to more arguing about the money.

He snuffed out the match and left, closing the door gently behind him.

The bank was dark. Shades had been drawn behind the

glass panes of the doors. He walked on past them, and past the big window that carried the bank's name. The small window of Samson's office was dark, too. The heavy drapes covered it. The whole building looked empty.

He knocked on the glass.

After a moment a dim glow appeared within the bank. He went back to the door then.

A key rattled in the lock. Then a bolt scraped and clicked. Finally the door opened and Millard Samson faced him. Samson was carrying a small desk lamp turned low. In a hushed, conspiratorial whisper he said to Todd, "Come in."

Todd stepped inside.

Samson turned the key in the lock. He didn't bother with the bolt. Holding the lamp up, he led Todd through the shadows to his office.

He set the lamp down on the desk, seated himself in the big chair behind it, and gestured for Todd to sit down across from him.

Todd felt too taut to sit. He stood looking expectantly at Samson.

Samson leaned back in the swivel chair. It was an indolent, self-possessed posture. But there was nothing indolent in his eyes. They were sharp and hard, glittering in the lamplight.

He was angry, Todd thought. But the anger showed only in his eyes. The rest of Samson's face was calm and soft. And that seemed wrong.

"Well?" Samson said.

"Ten thousand dollars."

"For Andy Groseille?"

Todd nodded. He wondered if Samson could have learned that Groseille would settle for five thousand. If Samson knew that Todd was trying to swindle him—

Todd gazed into the glittering eyes, trying to read the thought behind them.

Samson blinked. He glanced down at the top of the desk. It was cluttered with papers. Leaning forward, he put a hand on a small stack of envelopes tied together with twine. The motion was oddly slow and deliberate, as if he savored the moment. He picked up the packet and held it out to Todd.

With a sudden smile he said, "You know where Andy hid the copies of that story of his? In a *safe* place. In the bank!"

Todd eyed the envelopes. "Those?"

Samson chuckled. It was a hollow sound. A secretive amusement. "He left them here with me for safekeeping I had no idea what they might be at the time. After our talk this afternoon, I remembered them and took a look at them. Here. Go ahead, take them. Burn them if you want to."

Todd accepted the packet of envelopes. As he stuffed it into his coat pocket, he said, "This doesn't make any difference. Even if he has lost these, he can set the type again. He will. If I don't get back to him with the money soon, he'll print the whole thing in tomorrow's paper."

"And then you'll tell the rest of the story?" Samson said. "The part about my involvement?"

"If I have to go back to Groseille without that ten thousand, I'll tell it to him. I'm certain he could find room for another paragraph or two in tomorrow's paper."

"Ten thousand, you say?"

Todd nodded.

Samson tugged open a desk drawer and reached into it. His hand came out holding a banded wad of bills. He tossed it onto the desk. "That's ten thousand. Count it if you want to."

Todd was tempted to count it. He would enjoy the insult to Samson. But he wanted to get the hell out of the office. Away from Samson. Get it all over with. He riffled the bills to see that there were no blanks, no pieces of cut newspaper sandwiched in among the real bills. Groseille wouldn't find that amusing at all. But the bills all looked good. And it looked like there were enough of them.

"That's it," he said, slipping the money into his other coat pocket. "It's done."

"It's done," Samson agreed.

Todd started for the door.

He heard the click. And he knew the sound. It was the

catch of a gun sear. The small statement that a gun was cocked and ready to be fired.

The office door was closed. Flinging himself toward it, he grabbed the knob. Twisted. The door was opening and he was lunging through the doorway as a shot exploded the silence of the office.

He felt the impact as if something had kicked him in the side. It was a hard, jolting kick that threw him off balance. He sprawled beyond the doorway, rolling as he hit the floor.

Samson's second shot slammed into the floor where he had been. But he was already ducking behind a desk, putting its bulk between himself and the doorway.

He heard Samson mutter a curse, and he thought the gun must have been a two-shot kind, an over-under derringer or something of that ilk.

He had a gun himself. It was in the waistband of his trousers. But his coat and vest were buttoned over it. And his right arm wouldn't move. It hung numb, useless, from his shoulder. There was no pain, just numbness. But the arm wouldn't move.

On his knees, crouched behind the desk, he fumbled at the coat buttons with his left hand. One opened. Then another. The next refused. He jerked at it, popping it off. Then the fourth coat button. But the vest was another matter.

And somebody was banging at the door to the bank, shouting to know what was happening.

"Help!" Samson shouted from the depth of his office. He had doused the light. He was probably hiding in there, afraid Todd might be armed, afraid Todd was waiting beyond the door, gun in hand, ready for revenge.

Todd spat out a silent curse. He did have a gun. But he couldn't get at the damned thing. He couldn't get the damned vest unbuttoned.

There were more voices outside now. A crowd was gathering, growing excited.

Another shot echoed within Samson's office. Todd understood Samson had reloaded his sleeve gun and fired it to impress the audience outside.

The banging at the door increased, and he knew they were trying to break it open.

Samson fired another shot for effect and cried, "Look out! He's armed! Shoot to kill!"

Samson's attempt at murder had failed. Now he was cowering in his office, calling on others to finish the job for him. And they would probably be glad to do it.

Todd glanced around. He had to escape. But how?

The banging at the door became rhythmic. It was a heavy thudding now, as if the crowd outside had gotten a battering ram. The door couldn't last much longer.

Samson screamed for help again.

The hammering at the door continued.

Todd gave up trying to open the vest. He leaned back against the desk, trying to visualize the room as he had seen it earlier in the day. He thought there was only one door.

But maybe there was more than one way out.

He remembered the goggle-eyed clerk dipping a pen into an inkwell. A very large cut-glass inkwell. Rising onto his knees, he groped at the top of the desk with his left hand.

He found the inkwell. It was even heavier than he had expected. As he hefted it, ink spilled onto his hand.

Carrying it, he worked himself to the far end of the desk. Then to the wall. He rose and stood with his back pressed to the wall.

Another thud, and the door smashed open.

Outside there was a cheer of victory. Then sudden silence as the crowd realized there was still a man to be captured. A man who might be lurking in the darkness with a gun aimed at the broken door, ready to fire at the first one who rushed through it.

Poised, Todd waited. His right arm and most of his side were numb, but his legs seemed to be all right. He hoped to hell they would stay that way.

Someone outside shouted, "You! You in there! You don't have a chance. Come out with your hands up!"

Todd waited in silence.

"Help! Robbery!" Samson screamed.

A shadow moved. Someone was slipping into the bank. That would be Horne, Todd thought. The others outside would be watching, intent on Horne and what might happen inside.

Todd flung the inkwell.

The big front window shattered with a startling crash. Glass shards showered down with a sound of doomsday.

And Todd was running. Leaping through the window and running like all hell.

It was a fencer's leap, clean and neat. He landed in motion, dashing for the far corner while the men bunched at the bank door stood frozen, uncomprehending. He had almost reached the corner before the instant of shock passed and someone flung a shot at him.

It missed.

As he ducked around the corner there were more shots. He heard more shouting, a confused, cursing gabble that was finally broken by Horne's bellow.

"Goddammit, don't let him get away! Get the damn town surrounded! Bottle him up!"

Todd plunged into the alley that paralleled the main street. He knew men would be following him and more would be racing to cut him off. A clatter of hoofs told him that riders were heading out to the edges of town. There would be no escape that way. Horne would have him surrounded. He would have to go to ground.

He found the barn. The doors were pulled almost shut. He shoved one with his shoulder, slid past its edge, then closed it by leaning his back against it.

This was the carriage house where he had killed time during the afternoon. The scent of wet paint was still in the air. The odor of a hearse ready for a funeral.

Leaning against the door, Todd caught breath and listened.

Soon he heard faint noises in the alley. There was a murmur of voices and a screeching of rusty hinges. Men were searching for him.

The surge of strength that had brought him out of the bank, that had brought him this far, was fading fast. The numbness in his arm and side seemed to be spreading. His body didn't want to move.

He forced himself away from the door. Groping in the darkness, he found the hearse and traced his way to the front of it. His fingers located the fringe of the hammercloth. He tossed back the drape. With grunting effort, he pulled himself up onto the driver's step. It took more effort, exhausting effort, to squirm in under the bench seat. The space was small. There was barely room enough for him to squeeze himself in. Knees folded, back bent, lying on the uninjured side, he tugged the cloth down again.

It was a little piece of hell there under the seat and the heavy hammercloth. It was close and tight and stinking hot. Sweat and blood soaked him. The muscles that weren't numb cramped quickly. Now his body ached to move, begged to straighten and stretch.

He had to stay hidden. He knew that the searchers would come.

The silence was as thick and heavy as the heat. It was a black silence filled with the pounding of his own heart, the gasping of his breath. A suffocating silence.

It broke suddenly. The creak of the barn door was like a crash of thunder against the blackness. It startled him. Breath held tight in his aching chest, he listened to the soft scuffing of boots and the clearing of a throat. Then the murmur of cloth on cloth, the faint rustling of clothes, as the men moved within the barn.

"You look over yonder," one man said.

Todd guessed that there would be two of them. One with a lantern to do the searching. The other with a gun to protect him. He could see a dim suggestion of light through the fringes and moth holes of the hammercloth. He thought he could smell gun oil and man sweat. He thought he sensed fear in the scent.

Samson would have indentified him to them, and would have told them he was desperate, ready to kill. Samson would want them to shoot first. He would want Todd dead. He would desperately want Todd dead now.

At last the faint lantern light disappeared. The sounds faded. And the black silence was complete again. Suffocating him.

He lay counting his own heartbeats, forcing himself to let long minutes pass. Finally he could stand it no more. Shoving back the hammercloth, he sucked a breath and dragged himself from under the hearse seat.

The numbness that had shielded him from pain was abandoning him. As he moved, he felt the wound, sudden and vicious, a core of pain in his side jabbing long spears into the rest of his body. He couldn't stifle a groan as he dropped to the ground. He landed on his feet, but his knees folded. Sprawling on his face, he lay still.

Every muscle ached. Where the bullet had hit him, he felt on fire. For a while, he wondered what was the use—let them find him and kill him and be done with it.

No, dammit, no!

With his good hand braced, he got himself up off his face. Sitting, he rested awhile, then grabbed the wheel of the hearse and began to drag himself onto his feet. Slowly. Very slowly.

Finally he was standing, leaning against the wheel. Exhausted, he gasped for breath. His head was spinning, and the pain in his side was worse than a burning now. It pounded at him with every heave of his chest. He remembered another bullet, the fruit of a duel, and wondered why this was so much worse.

Because it was deeper, he supposed. Because it was killing him.

Then he remembered the doctor. There was always a doctor at a duel, ready to act instantly, always carrying morphine and laudanum to deaden pain.

There was cough syrup under the seat of the hearse. A bottle of very potent cough syrup.

Cautiously he released his grip on the wheel. He didn't fall. Slowly, trying not to worsen the pain, he reached under the seat. His hand found the bottle. He pulled the cork with his teeth, spat it out, and took a long swallow.

The alcohol kicked him in the stomach, then the head. He clung to the hearse, dizzy, almost sick. Then the warmth began to spread through his body. The dizziness eased. The pain began to fog.

He drank again, emptying the bottle.

CHAPTER 19

Todd didn't know how long he had been standing braced against the hearse. Perhaps minutes, perhaps hours. He didn't think he had actually been asleep, but he came to awareness suddenly, like a man who had dozed off for a moment against his will.

It was a hazy awareness. His mind felt as if it were a thing apart from his body, only distantly linked to it. The alcohol and opium of the cough syrup deadened feeling. The pain in his side was something far away, something his body was dreaming while his mind ranged.

Concentrating, he focused on how he had gotten there and what had happened. And what would happen.

He would die.

That thought seemed very clear. A simple truth, absolute and inevitable. He didn't want to die. But he didn't think there was a damned thing he could do about it. Even if the wound in his side didn't kill him, there were men hunting him with guns. If they captured him alive, he would be hanged.

So he was going to die and that was that. If he couldn't escape it, he had to accept it. But bedamned if he would die alone. Samson was murdering him, and Samson would pay for it.

How?

He wondered just when Samson had decided to kill him. Long before he arrived at the bank to pick up the money, he thought. Perhaps that afternoon, when he told Samson the swindle was sour. Perhaps back in New York when the whole deal was made. Samson wouldn't want loose ends left once it was all done. He might have planned all along to rid himself of the one man who could implicate him in the swindle.

Now Samson's plans were awry. As long as Todd was alive, Samson was in danger of exposure. Even if no one believed that Samson had intended murder, his part in the swindle could be proved. Todd could tell them where to look for that proof.

Todd asked himself what he would do now if he were Samson.

Prepare to run, he thought. Stand ready. If he heard Todd was dead, he could relax and return safely to his normal routine. If he heard Todd had been taken alive, he might still escape. Probably with a satchel full of money.

No. Todd wouldn't let that happen. He would stay alive long enough to see Samson dead.

Experimentally, he took a step away from the hearse. Despite the feeling of disassociation, his legs obeyed him. He tried moving his right hand. That was no good. The hand was no longer his. But the left hand still worked. Maybe one hand would be enough.

He fought open the vest and tugged the Remington from his waistband. The gun felt awkward in his left hand. He tried his thumb on the hammer. The action felt impossibly stiff. He wasn't certain he would be able to cock it. But when the time came, he would have to, and that was that.

Carrying the gun, he went to the door. He nudged it open a crack and looked out at the night. After the heavy darkness of the barn, the moonlight in the alley seemed very bright. He could see details easily. Barrels and crates behind buildings. Blank doors in blank walls. Lamplight in a back window.

No men.

Maybe the search was over.

He doubted that. But at least it had moved on to some other place. There was no one in sight here. He edged out into the alley. Working his way along the walls, he reached

the side street that crossed the alley. There he stopped with
his back pressed to a wall, and listened.

He could make out voices but not the words they spoke.
They seemed distant. He thought the people talking must be
well around the corner, perhaps all the way up at the main
street.

Moving with caution, he looked into the side street. It was
empty.

Lanterns glared at the corner of the main street. He could
see people bunched in their light. Not searchers but gossipers
intent on their talk. None of them were looking his way.

Poised, he drew a deep breath, then darted across the side
street. In the alley again, in the protective shadow of another
building, he leaned against a wall and rested.

There was no shouting, no sound of running. No one had
seen him. So far, so good.

After a moment, he moved on. And on, until he had
reached the end of the business district. He crept past a plank
fence that surrounded a back yard, and eased along the wall
of an outbuilding, and then ahead of him, across an open
field, he could see the looming bulk of Millard Samson's
house.

The windows were all dark, and he wondered if Samson
could have fled already. Maybe he hadn't waited to learn
what happened to Todd. Maybe he'd panicked and run.

Todd shook his head, answering himself that Samson
wouldn't run until he was positive that he had lost. No, he
would hang onto everything he had until the last possible moment.

Then Todd wondered if Samson was so confident of himself and his luck that he had simply gone home to bed.

Todd didn't dare try to cross the open field. Not when
there might be guards patrolling the outskirts of town
watching for him. He had to keep to cover. He would have to
work around the long way, through the brush that backed the
field and then up behind the shrubbery that surrounded Samson's yard.

He thought suddenly of Samson's maid and the stories that Don Edmund had hidden his horse in those bushes while he visited her. If a horse could be hidden back there, a man should be able to hide himself.

It was a long way around the open field, working through the overgrowth. By the time he reached Samson's shrubbery, he knew the effect of the cough syrup was wearing off. The pain in his side was getting nearer, sharper. His strength was running low.

Unsteadily, he shoved between the bushes. His face dripped sweat. Not simply the sweat of heat, but of exertion. His whole body felt soaked in it. He wondered if his side was still bleeding. He couldn't tell. There had been no way to plug the bullet hole. He couldn't reach that part of his back.

He would have to get this done quickly, he thought, or he would never finish it at all.

The house stood tall and formidable before him. The upstairs windows were closed to keep the unhealthy night air out of the bedrooms, but downstairs the windows had been left open to catch any small breezes that might blow through. That was luck. He dragged himself up onto the side veranda. There he rested awhile, leaning against the wall beside an open window.

Through the window he could see only vague shapes and dark shadows. He thought this was the study, where he had talked to Samson on his visit to the house. He tried to remember the layout of the room, but it blurred in his mind. Everything blurred for a moment, and he thought he had lost.

Not yet, he insisted to himself.

He had to go on. Determined, he faced the window. He couldn't just step over the sill. Not with his legs shaking the way they were, threatening to buckle under him. He had to seat himself on the sill and work one leg over at a time.

At last he was on his feet inside the room. He looked around, peering at the shadows, trying to pick out a path to the door. He thought the big desk was in his way.

With his good hand held out in front of him, he took one cautious step, then another. His hand found the edge of the desk. He leaned on it and walked around its end, then stepped away from it.

Suddenly he walked into something. Stumbling, he flung out his hand. He had rammed into a chair. It skidded at the thrust of his weight. He was falling on his face. And the chair was slamming into something else. He heard a clatter of glass, then a crash. The scent of kerosene filled his nostrils. He realized he had knocked over a lamp.

And he had lost his gun.

Lying on the floor, he groped for it. He felt the carpet as far as he could reach. He found only broken glass and the dampness of kerosene.

There were sounds overhead. The soft touch of feet on the floor above. The creaking of a board. Then a very faint spill of light in the next room, seeming to come down from the ceiling.

A woman's voice called, "Millard? Is that you?"

He thought she must be at the head of the stairs, holding out her lamp, looking down into the parlor. He heard the rustle of her dressing gown and the pat of her slippers on the steps. The light grew brighter as she brought the lamp downstairs.

He had to hide. But he couldn't move. Struggling, he got himself sitting up. His legs refused to do any more than that for him.

Galatea Samson came into view beyond the doorway, holding a reading lamp in her hand, frowning into the shadows.

"Millard?" she called. Her voice was tentative. Frightened.

Todd saw her go to the front door and test the knob. It was locked. She turned away from the door, facing into the darkened house, and called again, "Millard?"

A bit of breeze stirred the curtains at the open study window. It must have carried the kerosene scent to her. She sniffed the air and turned toward the study.

Todd tried again to move. Again his legs refused him. The

woman was approaching him. In a moment she would see him sitting helpless on the floor.

He called quietly to her, "Mrs. Samson?"

She flinched as if he had hit her. She halted in a moment of stark fear, her hand trembling. The light flickered, dancing shadows across the terror in her face. Her voice hushed and quavering, she asked, "Who is that? Who's in there?"

"Todd Fox."

"Who? Who are you? What are you doing there?"

He realized he had given her a name she wouldn't know unless she was party to her husband's scheme. Evidently she wasn't.

He told her, "James Todd. Remember? I came here—"

"Oh, yes!" It was a gasp of deep relief. The fear drained out of her. It was replaced by bewilderment. "What are you doing there? Why are you in the dark? Where's Millard?"

"Isn't he home yet?"

"No. Mr. Todd, what's going on?" She came into the doorway, her lamp held out before her.

The light touched Todd, and she started at the sight of him. Her mouth gaped and her eyes widened. The fear rushed back into her.

Long stains of blood smeared Todd's right trouser leg. His left hand was splashed blue with the ink he had spilled in the bank, and spattered red with blood. There was more blood on his face, where he had wiped at the sweat with his hand.

He gestured vaguely. "There was an accident."

"You're hurt!"

He nodded.

She knew James Todd as a gentleman. She saw him now, helpless and in need. Her fear faded. Setting the lamp on the desk, she reached a hand out to him. "Let me help you."

He accepted the hand. Hanging onto her, he managed to get his legs under him. A few stumbling steps took him to the chair behind the desk. He slumped into it.

"What happened, Mr. Todd?" she asked. "You're so—I'd better send for the doctor."

"No! No doctor."

"But you're bleeding."

"I'll be all right."

"What happened?"

"There was some trouble in town," he told her. "Some shooting. I'm afraid I was hit."

"How terrible! Oh! Was—" She hesitated. Her expression wasn't one of fear. It was strange, almost a look of hopeful anticipation. "Was Millard involved?"

"He wasn't hurt," Todd said. "I thought he would be home by now."

"No." Her voice was soft with the distraction of some private thought.

Leaning his head against the high back of the chair, Todd studied her from under heavy lids. Her face seemed very haggard, far older and wearier than it had been just a few days before. She looked used. Broken. As if something had happened that had sapped her emotional strength. Something she had wept over.

"It wasn't Peggy Landers," he mumbled.

She returned from the depth of her thoughts. Puzzled, she asked, "Did you say something about Peggy Landers?"

"She's gone," he said vaguely.

Her voice became the querulous, put-upon whine of a woman with servant problems. "Yes, and we only kept the one girl. We haven't replaced her yet. It's very awkward not having a servant around the house."

"Why did Samson dismiss her?" Todd asked.

"She was nothing but—" She stopped short and swallowed the anger that had been in her voice. "It hardly matters. She wasn't satisfactory. That's all."

Todd smiled slightly at his own thoughts. Things were beginning to fit together, to make a pattern.

Galatea Samson arched a brow at him. "Did you know Peggy?"

He gave a shake of his head. That was a mistake. The motion set his head to spinning. Clenching his eyes shut, he clutched the arm of the chair with his good hand and hung on.

He heard concern in her voice. "I think I should send for the doctor."

Struggling for strength, he forced his eyes open again. Sharply, he insisted, "No!"

"Really!" She frowned at him. Then a slyness came into her face. "Millard was involved in the shooting, wasn't he?"

"He's not hurt," he mumbled.

That wasn't what interested her. She said, "This is one of those 'private' matters, isn't it?"

He knew she meant "illegal." So she had suspicions about her husband's activities.

He didn't answer.

She took his silence as confirmation of her guess. Her face showed a mixture of distaste and satisfaction, as if she had learned something very unpleasant about an enemy.

Todd wondered where Samson was. Maybe on his way home now. He glanced around, hunting the gun he had dropped. He spotted it gleaming dully in the lamplight, just under the edge of the sideboard. It was far out of his reach.

The strength of the cough syrup had faded. The pain was sharp now, overwhelming him. The weight of the odds against him was an exhausting burden. He looked up at the decanter and glasses on the sideboard. Bright sparks of lamplight reflected deep within the liquor in the decanter. It looked very inviting. He thought maybe he would have done better drowning himself in a bottle than dying there like this.

There was no chance of taking Samson, no hope of winning. Not now, like this.

CHAPTER 20

Todd wanted a drink. And it sure as hell didn't seem to matter now. Maybe it would even help.

"Mrs. Samson, would you please be so kind—" His voice was weak. It broke on him. He caught a breath and went on. "Please be so kind as to spare me a little of your husband's brandy?"

"Of course."

She brought the tray with the decanter and glasses and set it on the desk. Todd reached for the decanter. His hand felt very heavy. It trembled. He knew he couldn't lift the bottle.

"Would you pour, please?"

"I should send for the doctor," she said as she tipped brandy into a glass. She poured a small, genteel drink and held the glass out to him.

It tried to slip through his fingers as he took it. He managed to hold onto it. There was nothing genteel in the way he downed the drink.

"More?" he asked.

She filled the glass again.

The brandy had a smooth fire, a strong fire that gave strength and burned away the sharp edge of the pain. He began to wonder if there might not be some hope after all.

"Millard should be home soon," she was saying.

Looking at her over the rim of the glass, he wondered about her relationship with her husband. It certainly wasn't a happy one. Perhaps she would be glad to be rid of him. But Galatea was a lady of fine family, of social prominence. She might fear a scandal more than she hated Millard Samson.

The brandy was working for him. His hand was steadier

now. He felt stronger. He thought he might be able to refill the glass himself. His fingers wrapped around the neck of the decanter. But as he picked it up, they slipped. The bottle hit the desk atilt, almost toppling.

She snatched at it, catching it before it could fall. Sternly she said, "You're badly hurt, Mr. Todd! You *need* the doctor!"

"No!" he snapped. More softly he said, "I need another drink."

As she poured it for him, she started to speak again. "I really do think—"

"*Quiet!*" he whispered harshly. He thought he had heard a sound. Something outside.

She cocked her head, listening.

There was a murmur of voices muffled by walls and distance. A heavy step sounded on the veranda. Then a key grated in the front door lock.

"That's Millard!" she said, apprehension and relief mingling in her voice.

Todd heard the door swing open. From where he sat, he couldn't see it. He heard Samson call, "Galatea?"

Todd couldn't see Samson, but Samson could see the light in the study. He would come this way.

Todd flung himself from the chair. Sprawling on the floor, he stretched his good hand toward the gun under the sideboard. His fingers locked over it, and he rolled onto his back. There was new strength in him now. Not just the heat of the brandy, but the fire of desperation.

Twisting, he sat up. The wall was behind him. He leaned against it, lifting the gun. His thumb found the hammer. With effort, he struggled it back. He heard the welcome click as the sear caught.

It was cocked. Ready.

Samson was coming toward the study. Todd could see him now, approaching the doorway. The line of sight was clear. Leveling the gun, Todd called, "Come on in, Millard! With your hands up!"

Samson saw Todd. And he saw the gun. His eyes narrowed. Slowly, he raised one hand. He had a satchel grasped in the other. He clung to it.

Galatea's mouth was agape. Her hands had gone to her breast. She stood taut, fearful, her eyes darting from her husband to Todd.

"Millard?" she gasped. "What's happening? What does he want?"

Samson looked at Todd and asked, "Money?"

"The truth," Todd said.

Samson laughed, and that was wrong. In the bank he had been afraid to poke his nose out of his office, afraid Todd might have a gun. Now Todd did have a gun and Samson wasn't afraid.

"*You?*" Samson said, his tone mocking. "*You* want the truth? You have the truth on those press proofs in your pocket, Mr. *Fox*. The truth is the blood you're spilling on my carpet. You're losing a lot of it. You're almost too weak to hold up that pistol. The truth is that without my help, you are a dead man, Mr. Fox."

Todd understood Samson's calm then. Samson thought he had come desperate for escape, meaning to demand help at gun point. Samson thought the gun was more bluff than threat.

"With *your* help I am a dead man," Todd said. "As dead as Don Edmund."

Galatea gasped at the name. Todd glanced at her from the corner of his eye. Her haggard face was ashen pale.

He looked quickly back at Samson. "It wasn't Peggy Landers who Edmund came here to see, was it? It was your wife, wasn't it? That's why you killed Edmund, isn't it?"

"*Millard!*" Galatea's voice was filled with shock.

"That's two murders," Todd said, thinking of himself as the second victim. "Are there any more?"

Samson started with surprise. "Two? You know about Andy Groseille?"

"What about Groseille?" Todd asked with a frown. "You killed him, too?"

"You didn't know?"

"Of course you killed him," Todd said, remembering the still figure on the cot in the newspaper office. Groseille hadn't been sleeping. He had been dead. "Of course. When the story came out, *I'd* be blamed for his murder, too. You would be completely clear. Groseille wouldn't begin to wonder where I could get five thousand dollars, and who in Stick City might be my partner in the game."

"*Five* thousand? You told me *ten!*" Samson exploded, his face reddening. "You tried to swindle me!"

"Fair enough, don't you think? You tried to *kill* me." Todd heard his own voice fading as he spoke. He was dizzy again. It was taking all the strength he had to keep the gun aimed at Samson. He thought he would have to get this over with quickly, before he passed out.

The pistol trembled in his hand as he tightened his forefinger on the trigger. The spring felt heavy. Far too heavy. It refused to yield to the weak pressure of his finger.

He couldn't pull the damned trigger.

"No!" Samson protested. Dropping the satchel, he spread both hands open in a plea-like gesture. He took a step toward Todd as if he meant to beg.

That was wrong, Todd thought as he struggled against the impossible trigger.

Samson moved suddenly. He lunged to the side, one hand sweeping toward the lamp on the desk. Catching it, he flung it at Todd.

In the same instant, the trigger gave to Todd's pull. The hammer fell. A blast of sound and powder smoke filled the study. But Todd knew the shot had gone wild.

The glass lamp shattered against the wall above Todd's head. Flaming oil showered down on him. With a sudden surge of strength, he threw himself full length on the floor and rolled. Rolling, he crushed the little flames that snatched at his clothing.

Behind him, oil spread down the wall and onto the carpet. The flames raced along it, filling the room with their wild light.

Galatea screamed.

The pain of the wound lashed through Todd, sapping the last of his strength. He lay still, prone, his face turned toward Samson. He couldn't move. He could barely draw breath. His vision hazed as he looked at Millard Samson.

By the flame-light, Samson's face was a distorted play of shadows, a devil mask.

Samson's right shoulder bobbed. An over-under derringer sprang from his sleeve into his hand. He aimed it at Todd's head.

Todd's hand was empty. His pistol lay on the floor. He could see it but he knew he couldn't reach it. He couldn't move.

"*Damn you!*" Galatea screeched. Ducking, she scooped up Todd's pistol. She swung the muzzle toward her husband. "*You killed Don!*"

The small, sudden roar of the pistol was very loud within the walls of the study.

Todd thought he heard something like a man's voice shouting at the instant of the shot. Then there was another roar, echoing the first.

Galatea jerked back. A small spot appeared on the front of her dressing gown. Staggering, she lifted a hand to it. She covered it with her palm, as if she meant to hide it. Her face was very pale. Blank.

"You—" Her voice was a whisper. The pistol slid out of her fingers. As gracefully as if she were making a much-practiced curtsey, she crumpled to the floor.

A man was shouting.

The voice was coming from the window behind Todd. He thought he recognized it. The voice of Deputy Charlie Horne. But that was impossible.

Samson was twisting, firing again, sending a wild slug toward the window. And then he was flinging himself back against the wall, in the corner behind the sideboard. He crouched there, hidden from the window.

Todd knew then that Charlie Horne was at the window. Samson was hiding from his gunsight.

The fire was spreading. It ran across the carpet from the wall, finding the spot where the lamp Todd broke by accident had spilled oil. Greedily, it ate at the stained carpet.

Lying on the floor, Todd could see past the end of the desk. Beyond the flames, he could see Samson at the end of the sideboard. And he could see the satchel that Samson had dropped. It sat upright near Galatea's body. She had fallen with one arm outstretched, as if she were reaching for the satchel.

It was full of money, Todd thought. Samson would have cleaned out the bank vault, in case he had to run. That would be his escape fund. Probably mostly bank notes. They would be light, easy to carry.

Horne was calling through the window, pleading with Samson to give up a useless battle. But Samson had been carrying extra loads in his pocket for the derringer. He was busy fingering them into the gun.

Todd struggled for the strength to move himself. He fought the pain, the weakness. Gasping breath, he dragged himself across the carpet, toward the flames.

He had to see this finished. And he wasn't sure he had much more time. There was a darkness hovering close behind him. It wanted to swallow him. If it did, he was afraid that would be that.

Bedamned if he'd die without seeing Samson go down first.

At the corner of the desk, he managed to haul himself up onto his knees. He could see Samson snapping shut the derringer. The gun was ready to be used again.

Todd threw himself forward across the flames. He fell on his face, his body partly in the fire. His arm was thrust out ahead of him, his hand reaching for the satchel. His fingers caught it. Tugged at it.

He was trying to roll. It seemed that an eternity passed as

he struggled unsuccessfully. And then he was moving, rolling out of the fire, dragging the satchel into it.

Samson saw him.

Samson's eyes widened. The fire reflected in them, burning as if there were little flames behind the shining pupils.

For an instant, Samson was motionless, appalled as he saw the flames nuzzling around the satchel.

Then, suddenly, he screamed.

Slamming to his feet, he flung a wild shot toward the window. As he grabbed for the bag of money, he emptied the other barrel of the derringer at Todd.

Todd felt the slug snatch at his sleeve. He felt the thud as it smashed into the floor.

Samson snatched up the satchel and wheeled toward the doorway.

Horne's shot hit him in the back.

It sent him spinning through the doorway, sprawling into the parlor.

Todd saw him fall. And then there was only darkness.

CHAPTER 21

Todd became aware of hands pulling at his body. There was a voice. It was Horne's. "Come on, man! Wake up! You've got to get out of here!"

With surprise, Todd realized that he was still alive. Gasping, choking on the smoke that filled the study, he struggled to accept the help of the hands.

There were flames all around him, lapping at the desk, nibbling the curtains, streaking up the walls. The air was thick and hot. Hotter than the badlands. Hotter than he had ever felt it before.

Horne was pulling him onto his feet. Horne's arms were around him, shoving him toward the window. He was tumbled through it, then hauled to his feet again and dragged off the veranda into the clean, clear night air.

It felt cool outside. Very pleasantly cool, and a little damp, as if it might rain. Rain was good. He couldn't remember why, but he wanted rain desperately.

He saw faces all around him. The firelight from the burning house tinted them. Devilishly staring faces. And an awed muttering of voices. In the distance, a bell was clanging frantically.

Horne's hands dragged him past the faces toward a large tree. They lowered him to the ground to sit with his back against the trunk of the tree.

A fresh little breeze touched his cheek tenderly. It was soothing, like a woman's caress. He thought of Asia McRae. She was safe now. Samson could never steal Pitchfork now.

He heard Horne asking, "You hurt bad?"

"I'm not dead," he mumbled. Still thinking of Asia, he realized he was caught. The truth would come out. She would learn it all. He almost wished he were dead.

Horne scanned the crowd. "Is the doctor around here anywhere?"

Someone called back, "I'll fetch him!"

Horne hunkered at Todd's side. "You got a hell of a lot of explaining to do, Mr. Todd. Or is it rightly Mr. Fox?"

So Horne knew already, Todd thought. He wondered how the deputy could have found out so quickly. A way occurred to him. He asked, "You found Groseille's body?"

"Yeah."

"And the story?"

"Yeah."

"Samson killed him," Todd said, not expecting Horne to believe it. He expected Horne to accuse him of the murder.

But Horne said, "I know. I heard it all."

"Heard it?"

Horne nodded.

"How?" Todd asked.

"Nothing that's been going on around here lately has set right with me," Horne said. "I never did think that Cole McRae killed Don Edmund, but I couldn't figure who did. Then that bank holdup Millard tried to give me just didn't set right at all. Millard didn't act right. I set a posse onto your tail, like was my duty, but I stuck to Millard myself. I walked him home. Then I began snooping around the house. I was kinda wondering what he had tucked into that satchel he fetched home from the bank."

"Money," Todd said.

"Money," Horne agreed. "We got it out of the fire and it was purely stuffed with money . . ."

For an instant, Todd lost the thread of Horne's words. He felt himself slipping back into the darkness. He was falling. Dying.

But he didn't want to die.

Fighting the dizziness, he got his eyes open again. He

found the question he wanted to ask. "If you were there, why the hell didn't you stop him sooner?"

"I was listening outside that study window, but I didn't dare take a look through it for fear I'd show myself. I wanted to hear the whole of it before I busted in on him. I didn't know nobody was waving guns around. It wasn't until Miz Calatea started screaming and I heard shooting that I knew I had to move quick."

"You might have saved her," Todd muttered.

"I know," Horne's voice was low and sorrowful. "But there's times a man's foresight ain't damn near as good as his hindsight."

That was true, Todd thought. Too damned true.

And then the doctor was there, pushing through the crowd. He dropped to his knees at Todd's side. A bystander lit a match to give him more light. He scowled at the blood.

Gravely he said, "I've got to get this man to my infirmary."

"I'll get Samson's buggy." Horne rose and started off.

"Deputy," Todd called after him. "Am I under arrest?"

Horne looked back. "I don't know. Did you do anything illegal here in this county?"

"No," Todd said hopefully.

Horne shrugged.

"Then I can leave on the coach tomorrow?" Todd was thinking of Asia again. And of escaping having to face her.

"Not likely," Dr. Durfee told him. "I don't think you'll be doing anything but resting in bed for a while."

"But I've got to leave tomorrow!" He made an effort to rise. "I've got to get away . . ."

The night turned red suddenly. Red, and then black as the darkness swallowed him.

He was sitting up in the bed in the doctor's little infirmary, his torso wrapped in bandages and his arm in a sling. Sitting trapped, helpless, as Amos McRae came through the door.

Cole followed Amos in.

For a frightened instant, Todd thought Asia would be there too. But she wasn't.

Relieved, yet still afraid, he faced the two men.

Amos spoke, his voice demanding, "What the hell is this you were telling Asia about the railroad?"

"Sir?" The question startled Todd. He had been expecting accusations and condemnation.

"When she stopped me of taking that mortgage with Samson, she said you told her the railroad was coming to Dadeston."

"Yes."

"Without us doing anything special to get it here?" Cole asked.

Todd nodded.

Amos scowled at him. "The rest of it, all that talk about you building a spa and everything, that was all lies? All a swindle you and Samson cooked up between you to get money off me?"

Todd felt an urge to explain, to tell Amos the idea was all Samson's and that he, Todd, had been forced into it. But Samson hadn't forced him. He had made his own decision. He swallowed and said, "Yes."

"Then why did you tell Asia to stop me from getting the mortgage?"

"Samson," Todd answered. "He wanted that mortgage so he could foreclose it and take Pitchfork away from you. With the railroad coming into the area, he thought a spa at your spring really would be a successful business. He meant to get the spring and build a spa, and run you out of business for personal reasons, all at the same time."

"Uh huh," Amos said to himself. He turned to Cole. "See? I told you the damned thing was a good idea."

"Hell, I don't know anything about spas," Cole grumbled.

"Neither do I," Amos said. He looked at Todd again. "Do you really know anything about them? According to that piece of Andy Groseille's, you been all over Europe, hobnobbing with them society folk. You really know about spas?"

"Some," Todd said. "I agree that your spring would be a good site for one. Nothing to compare to Saratoga, but a nice small resort."

"Uh huh," Amos said again. "Look here, Todd—uh—Fox—whatever the hell your name really is—according to Charlie Horne, you damned near got yourself killed. How come you'd do that instead of sticking with Samson and taking the money?"

Todd couldn't voice his reasons. He said, "I changed my mind."

"Why?"

"I didn't want to see you lose Pitchfork to a bastard like Samson."

"Why not?" Amos insisted.

Todd said, "What the hell difference does it make? It's all over now."

"I want to know!"

"My reasons are none of your damned business!"

Amos turned to Cole. "What do you think?"

Cole shrugged.

"Well, I'll tell you," Amos said to Todd. "I think you got a decent streak in you. That's what. Do you think you could stay honest with us? Keep your hands in your own pockets and work with us to build this thing in exchange for a fair share of the profit?"

"Sir?"

"You want to help build it or not?" Amos snapped.

"Pa means the spa," Cole said. "A bunch of us got together and talked it over, and we figured it might be a good idea to build it just the way you said. Bring in new folk and money and—"

"We don't know nothing about spas around here," Amos interrupted. "We need somebody as does."

Cole nodded in agreement.

"You're a thief by trade, mister," Amos continued. "I don't trust you any further than I'd trust any horsethief or long roper I ever done business with. But there's damned few men who never did anything dishonest. I've knowed some wild young fellers who ran a cinch ring or threw a long rope or even stopped a coach or two, but they eventually got some sense in their heads and settled down to be real decent folk. Maybe you could do the same if you put your mind to it. You interested?"

For a long moment, Todd stared at him, comprehending the offer Amos was making. It took a lot of effort to say, "No."

Amos seemed more than simply surprised. He looked actually shocked. And very disappointed.

"Why not?" he asked.

Todd just shook his head.

"It's on account of Asia, ain't it?" Cole said.

Todd said nothing. But the answer was in his face.

"Hell," Amos grunted. "This whole thing is Asia's idea. I mean about asking you to take over building the spa."

"Sir?"

"She said for us to fetch you back to the ranch to heal up from that wound," Cole said. "She told us we shouldn't take no for an answer."

Amos added, "She said for us not to let you get away, not until she gets a chance to know you more. She says she wants to find out just who you really are, and whether you're really the man she's got a notion you are."

Cole nodded.

"Are you?" Amos asked.

Todd didn't know. He didn't know who or what he might be behind the masks he had worn so much of his life.

He looked from Amos to Cole. They knew what he had been, what mask he had worn, and they were willing to take a chance on him.

So was Asia.

"Yes," he said.